"Intense visions abound in Christopher X. Shade's OF MARSEILLE. Well-developed characters, finding themselves in a landscape that is both beautiful and troubling, come to Marseille in search of many things—a chance to prove themselves, an adventure, a last hurrah. But what they find within is deeply more meaningful and surprising."
—**Chantel Acevedo**, author of *The Distant Marvels* and *The Living Infinite*

"THE GOOD MOTHER OF MARSEILLE is a beautiful and memorable debut, a melancholy tale of both lost and found, a love letter to the night-lights of France, a movable feast for this 21st century."
—**Scott Cheshire**, author of *High as the Horses' Bridles*

"No single viewpoint can take in a city like Marseille, marked up by too many cultures to count. So Christopher X. Shade provides us with a kaleidoscope, quite ingenious, in which shapes and colors young and old, native and foreign, exotic and run of the mill, tumble across one another. I dare you to look away."
—**John Domini**, author of *MOVIEOLA!*

"THE GOOD MOTHER OF MARSEILLE is a luminous, taut, utterly absorbing first novel. Part American expat novel à la *The Sun Also Rises*, the cast of characters also includes American tourists and French natives parallel playing out their dreams and sorrows on the stage of this gritty French port city. Shade is a compassionate observer of the human dilemma, his feel for place commanding, his story first-rate. I read it in one gulp."
—**Lesley Dormen**, author of *The Best Place to Be*

"THE GOOD MOTHER OF MARSEILLE by Christopher X. Shade is a painfully beautiful novel, infused with peril and propelled by suspense. In powerful prose, Shade renders a complex mosaic of a city's underbelly. These interlocking portraits of characters on the edge, barely hanging on, are filled with struggle—people who feel very real, confronting loss, doubtful futures, and their own existential fears."
—**Clifford Garstang**, author of *What the Zhang Boys Know* and *In an Uncharted Country*

"Using Marseille, France, as his canvas, Shade paints a cast of characters who, by their human interactions, invite the reader to repeatedly ask: Is it choice or fate that "leads us to the places we don't expect to be?" If you want to delve into what it means to be human, when so many are facing loneliness and loss, then THE GOOD MOTHER OF MARSEILLE is your invitation."
—**Elena Georgiou,** author of *The Immigrant's Refrigerator* and *Rhapsody of the Naked Immigrants*

THE GOOD MOTHER OF MARSEILLE

Christopher X. Shade

Paloma Press, 2019

ALSO FROM PALOMA PRESS:

Blue by Wesley St. Jo & Remé Grefalda
Manhattan: An Archaeology by Eileen R. Tabios
Anne with an E & Me by Wesley St. Jo
Humors by Joel Chace
My Beauty is an Occupiable Space by Anne Gorrick & John Bloomberg-Rissman
peminology by Melinda Luisa de Jesús
Close Apart by Robert Cowan
One, Two, Three: Selected Hay(na)ku Poems by Eileen R. Tabios, translated into Spanish by Rebeka Lembo (Bilingual Edition)
HAY(NA)KU 15 edited by Eileen R. Tabios
Humanity: An Anthology edited by Eileen R. Tabios

PALOMA PRESS
San Mateo & Morgan Hill, California
Publishing Poetry+Prose since 2016
www.palomapress.net

for Paige

CONTENTS

PART ONE

PART TWO

PART ONE

Noémie

Three years in, and Noémie still couldn't get a good night's sleep in Marseille's train station quarter. She couldn't leave the windows open because there was too much street noise. When the windows were closed, her bedroom was too hot. All night she was opening and closing the windows.

A Québécoise, she couldn't get used to the heat. The heat kept her awake. The night air outside was the same as inside. Lying awake, she worried that the next day would be hotter than the day before. Marseille, a bouillabaisse stew left on simmer. Distasteful, but it was hers. Young people at all hours of the night drank in the streets, cajoled each other, threw insults, sang, shouted declarations of love up at the windows. None of those shouts were for her. It was only a trick to get a woman, any woman, to come to a window. Traffic congestion on the boulevards sputtered and growled, and emitted the suffocating odor of exhaust.

A noise machine in the room broke ocean waves again and again. It was supposed to lull her to sleep. Instead all night she lay awake trying to parse the noise of the machine from the noise of the quarter.

An oscillating fan pushed warm air at her. Where the fan did not push air in the room, the air did not move. She could not leave the bedroom door open. If she left the door open, her hot dog Chinelo would stick his nose in the room, wander in, and then jump up on the bed but she would not have a dog on her bed, not even Chinelo.

Noémie took Chinelo out for walks in the quarter, day and night, on the narrow streets around the Jardin Labadié. On this night, there seemed to be no one else out. But she could hear the noise of people inside their apartments. It was a constant clamor that rose to an uproar and then broke, like an amplified version of her noise machine, with the agitation of a people who are discontent but at least have found one another. The noise was distinctly of this place. Montreal had not been like this. Noémie was tense, walking these streets. She could see these other people of Marseille in low windows, always together, like new friends in each other's company, carousing. Probably they didn't know that they could be seen as they were by her, that they were regarded with the bitterness that Noémie felt. For them, everything was working out. For them, everything was easier. She felt angry whenever she saw them in their windows as she walked, as Chinelo went ahead on the leash and paused to sniff things and was pulled and seemed annoyed of the leash. She called him Chino as they walked, sometimes Chi-chi, sometimes Choo-choo because he looked like a little train.

On this one-way street, some cars were parked facing the wrong direction. This was the way of Marseille. No one followed the rules. Noémie had come to expect this after hard years of daily melees. Money was hard to come by. She scraped together a living by translating technical documents from French to English for big French companies, work that came to her through recruiters. This work was dull and tedious because it had to be precise. It got in the way of what she was there to do, her dissertation. When she fell behind on bills she begged recruiters for more work. Sometimes she could get them to pay in advance. Hard seemed to be the way for everyone she knew in Marseille. Hard was simply the way of Marseille, in every way, big and small. But it was worth it. She felt this way and was sure that every other resident felt this way. There was no other place for her. She had made Marseille her place now.

In all of the noise, Noémie heard a peal of church bells that made her anxious about the late hour. She did not feel in danger for any reason other than the late hour. She could take care of herself. She was tough as nails, a man had once told her. He was a Michigan man she'd dated here in Marseille for a short time. He'd pulled away from her, more quickly than she'd expected, and then it wasn't long before he'd left Marseille and was absent from her life. She didn't think she was tough as nails. She hurt. She bled as easily as everyone else. A knife could cut her the same as anyone else. A strong man could physically overpower her, if she wasn't careful. Only she could outsmart them all. She was aware that this was not the safest place to be walking at night, on this street where lights did not do enough to dispel shadows, for anything might happen in Marseille. Anything might happen, just when one least expected it.

Also on this street there was an occasional parked van in which a prostitute worked, probably, for this was not uncommon, and it seemed to Noémie that some of tonight's street noise came from these vans. But she could not be certain of it. It was possible that all of the prostitutes were alone, like her, on a night like this.

Noémie rounded a corner and was going past an apartment building when glass shattered at her feet. As if her step had somehow made a glass thing explode. In the next instant more glass exploded at her feet. She didn't grasp what was happening. It startled Chinelo, too. At the end of the leash Chinelo leaped in surprise and yipped.

A bottle fell close to her face, and shattered at her feet. Bottles were falling from high up. Someone was dropping beer bottles from a fourth story window. She couldn't see who it was. If one hit her on the head, it might kill her. If one hit Chinelo, it might kill him.

Another bottle fell.

Noémie shouted in French up at the windows, "What are you doing? Stop! We are down here! What do you think you are doing?"

This way, this attitude, of not giving a thought to how it might be for others, was what Noémie had come to expect in Marseille. She believed that the people up at those windows had no intention of hurting anyone. It simply did not occur to them that they might be in the wrong. They were drinking and tossing empties out the window. In the moment, it meant nothing to them. It could not possibly be of any consequence, and later they would not even be able to recall what they'd done.

After she shouted up at the windows, no more bottles fell. Broken glass was all around so she picked up Chinelo. Then she saw blood at her feet. And blood on her hands. And blood on Chinelo. A shard of glass had gone into Chinelo's neck. Chinelo was bleeding badly.

She had to get him to the animal hospital, the clinique vétérinaire. It was several blocks away, and there was nothing to do but run as fast as she could with Chinelo in her arms through the streets up rue Jean de Bernardy for some blocks and across rue Louis Grobet for more blocks to the corner of the boulevard. She kept pressure on Chinelo's neck as well as she could with her wet hands. He was making a noise as she ran, a sad whine. He was in pain and afraid. He might be dying. She wept, "Chi-chi!" and held him tight. She pushed her way through the doors of the clinic, shouting for help. The workers broke away from sports on the TV. They took Chinelo out of her arms and treated him. The glass shard had just missed the artery. Chinelo had very nearly been killed.

It was the middle of the night when Noémie returned, with a bandaged Chinelo in her arms, to the place where the bottles had been dropped. When glass crunched beneath her shoes, she looked up at the fourth story window. Chinelo began to whine quietly in her arms. She called up, not unpleasantly, for the one who'd dropped the bottles. She tried not to sound as furious as she was feeling. She called up a few times, and at the building door she rang apartments, pushing the buttons again and again, but no one answered. She shouted up at them that they'd almost killed her dog. And it had cost a lot of money. It had cost her more than a month's rent to save him. They had almost killed him. And what then? What if they had killed her Chinelo? She said the police would come. She said she would call the police. She kicked at the broken glass.

She went straight home. Chinelo went to his place on the sofa and crawled under the blankets so that only his nose could be seen. Noémie phoned the police. She told the man on the other end what had happened, how she and her dog had almost been killed, and how she had rushed her injured dog to the hospital. Was that a TV she was hearing? Was he watching TV? Was he even listening to what she was saying? She and her dog had almost been killed.

He noted that she was Canadian. He explained that he could tell from her French that she was Canadian.

"I am American," she said, "on a doctoral program from a major American university."

"A student," he suggested.

She said they had almost killed her dog.

Another man came on the phone. "There is a match," he said.

"A what?"

"A football match."

"I have no patience for this," she said. Those people at the window had broken the law. It was a fourth story window. They had almost killed her dog. If a bottle had hit her, it would've killed her. A falling bottle might kill someone. Someone must make the people at the window understand that they cannot do this.

She said all this to the police, and she gave them the location. She said they must come to the place where it had happened and do something. They asked for the location. She told them, and told them again, because she did not believe they were writing it down. She said, "These people at the window committed a crime. It is a violence. You must do something."

She arranged to meet the police there. She went with Chinelo in her arms and waited. A light was on. Whoever did this was still there. She went around to some vans on the street and knocked on the doors. She could not see inside the vans. She could not hear anything happening in the vans, but she felt sure that prostitutes were in there, in at least some of these vans. She called out to the prostitutes: Did you see? The police are coming. Will you tell them what you saw?

Chinelo whined in her arms. No one else answered.

In Montréal it had been the same: neighbors did not open their doors. Most of the time no one was there to help them. Sometimes police came, and sometimes the police took her father away. Her father never came back sober. He never remembered what he'd done. He was not violent when he was not drinking. The drinking brought out the worst of him. One night her father walked out of the house and did not come back because that night somewhere along the way when he was drinking he punched a man who fell, hit his head, and died. The newspapers told a different story: the deceased had been dragged some distance, and had been found with the blow to the head and also a broken arm and gashes on the shoulder and face where the flesh had been torn away with teeth. Her father was incarcerated.

Then she and her sister were alone with her mother. Noémie was a teenager, her sister an early teen. It wasn't long before her mother began to sour things. Her mother's drinking made it worse: when there was no man to push away, she said hateful things to her daughters.

Her mother now lived alone outside of Montréal in one of the apartment houses along the St. Lawrence river. Noémie could only imagine how the apartment must be after her mother's years there alone, how much in disrepair the apartment would be, how musty, how empty, how foul with resentment. There would be no family photos on the walls. No sign of others. But really Noémie could not know. It had been years since she'd visited her mother—how many years? Many years, but not enough. Noémie would not go back. She did not expect to ever go back.

Noémie's younger sister lived near the neighborhood where they'd spent their childhood, on an edge of Plateau-Mont-Royal. Noémie didn't talk to her now. They'd had too many arguments. Their views on men had forced them apart. With men, her sister had always been giving and hopeful. Noémie had always been telling her, I told you so. Her sister was now a single mother, with the father of her child in prison, that man also unable to control the violent animal of himself that raged within. Noémie did not know if he was now in or out of prison, the same as their own father. These had been angry and violent drinking men, more angry when drinking, drinking more when angry, not unlike all the other men in the world as Noémie saw it.

Even her adviser back at the university was like this, the one American male she had phone calls with, her doctoral program adviser. She would not use the word mentor, she preferred the word adviser. He was an older man named Joe Gray. She did not use the word doctor with this man as all the others did, as was the way of these people who populated universities, these people, these people who competed against her and who never expected her to succeed but really all of her life had been this way and she showed them all, every time. Once on the phone with him she'd heard ice knocking in a glass. It was a sound that she knew well and would always recognize in the instant that she heard it. After that, she did not trust that he would be sober on the phone. Sometimes he raised his voice, shouting at her, trying to be stern. He didn't understand all that it meant to raise his voice in the ways that he did. It was a form of violence. And so she had no respect for him. But for now, he was useful. To stay in the doctoral program, she needed someone in the department on her side, and Gray would do.

Gray told her that she'd been working on her doctorate for too many years. Her research phase had been completed years ago. He told her there was no reason for her to be in Marseille. She wouldn't have all these money concerns if she returned to the university, to the United States, where she could live on campus and finish it.

But she wouldn't leave Marseille now, not for Montréal, and not for the university. Not for the university's green lawns and old trees. Not for Montreal's summer terraces in the Plateau, or for its winter ice skating at the Old Port. No, she wouldn't leave Marseille now, not for any of those places that others told her to live. Not even for the glow of Paris. Noémie had given up everywhere else. Marseille would be hers. She expected it to be. Already, she acknowledged it to be so. Marseille was her bouillabaisse stew. She could contend with its simmer, its daily threats of eruption.

Still Noémie waited just down the street from where there was the broken glass all over the sidewalk. For a while she held Chinelo in her arms, but then put him down, away from the glass, and with the leash did not let him go far. The police never came, and it was not long before the light went out at the fourth story window.

2

Harvey

The next morning, Noémie walked the bandaged Chinelo only as far as the street with the broken glass. She picked up Chinelo and held him in her arms. Embittered, she stared up at the fourth story window and at the street around her. She shook her head in disgust, and inwardly resolved to never forgive them, all of them. This had really set her back. To pay the bills, not just this month, but in the coming months, she would need more translation work. Already, those hours were too much. The work to get the work was too much. But it was what she would have to do—because of them, at the fourth story window. She spat on their street. Them! She turned, set down Chinelo, and walked him another way.

While Noémie wanted to stay in Marseille, Harvey Saunders did not want to stay. He and his wife Beverly had come to see the sights, which were nice to see, but what he really wanted was to get back home. Marseille was a pit stop on their tour. Not so for Noémie. She considered Marseille her place of residence, with reluctance, because the place was not perfect. But officially Noémie was not a resident. It was the university that sponsored her residency papers. Harvey and Beverly had planned to stay only a few nights. They were renting a room from a family. This morning they were in Marseille's Cathedral de Saint-Marie-Majeure. They were far, far away from their home in Alabama, a ranch style house they'd owned for many years in a neighborhood of houses that were all a little bit different while really all about the same. A short drive from their house lived their daughter. She was in a split-house rental with her own daughter Alex who'd just turned eleven.

Harv wore the camera strap over his shoulder. When he was not shooting, the heavy camera hung under his arm at his ribs. In the church he shot photos of everything. Statuary. Religious objects. He used the small tripod from his daypack for long exposure shots. He hit stained glass with the flash to capture both the colors and the interior stonework. The brightness of the flash hurt his eyes, though hurt was not the right word. It was more of a nudge. It was an urgent but gentle tap on the head. As if to say, *you're standing too far out on the street and there's a bus coming.* Years from now, or sooner, the pictures would be for Bev, and for their daughter and granddaughter. Harv would not be able to see the pictures. He would not be able to see anything. He was glad to know this in advance, to know that a monster of illness was about to pounce on him. Illness was a monster that out of nowhere jumped on you with its claws out.

They were touring Europe because his sight was failing. The doctor had called it *retinitis pigmentosa*. It was not exactly clear to him why they'd come to Marseille from Paris. Really it had been Bev's idea. They'd arrived by train the day before, a direct train from Paris.

First there had been Amsterdam. To get to Amsterdam they'd driven across Alabama over to the big Birmingham airport and then changed planes in New York City. From New York City they'd flown directly to Amsterdam, arriving the next morning, where they'd mainly toured the museums for three days. And then they'd taken a train to Paris. The train from Paris to Marseille had been an easy trip, even delightful, with red wine and stinky cheese and torn baguette and, out the windows, green and yellow fields and rolling green hills dotted with distant little houses. Now whenever they were ready they would be leaving Marseille by train for the next stop, which would be Barcelona, except Harv hadn't yet agreed to when they would leave for Barcelona, and Bev was leaving this mostly up to him, to a degree. Probably they'd pinned Marseille to their itinerary simply because it was on the way to Barcelona and she'd read somewhere that the little wooden ships hanging in the Notre-Dame de la Garde were a must-see. Whatever the reason they were in Marseille now, it didn't matter so much, except that there was not a lot of time to see things.

Harv was trying to steady the pace. Though there was not a lot of time, he didn't want to rush. Rushing would not get him home sooner, that much he knew. He hadn't done a lot of traveling, and neither had Bev. They'd been married thirty-odd years. For him there was only the bit of time overseas he'd done in the Navy, in his youth before marriage, when he'd spilled down with fellow seamen into foreign ports to drink and gamble and buy sex. The Navy hadn't taught him a thing about how to travel. But back home he had a close friend and neighbor who'd been around the world, and this fellow had told him to stay longer in fewer places, to remember to keep slowing things down, to savor things. Don't be too hasty, he'd said. And so after Harv and Bev visited some of the sights in Marseille—on this side of the harbor a walk all through the old quarter, Le Panier, all of its steep stone steps and narrow streets, and a visit to this cathedral of Saint-Marie-Majeure—and were on their way to a nearby small museum where they understood there to be paintings of scenes of this area, Harv felt that they were sightseeing too fast and though they could've kept going he suggested that they take a table where they happened to be at the time, going through the Place de Lenche, at an ice cream shop, Le Glacier du Roi. They took a table with a view between buildings and of the old port and in the distance of the Notre-Dame de la Garde church up on the hill.

They ordered coffee and ice creams but Harv could not understand the server well, so really he had no idea what they were going to get. And it didn't matter what it would be. Already this seemed a special place and experience and it would be hard to break that spell. When the ice cream arrived they were enormous heaps of hard vanilla ice cream in a chocolate shell, each with a butter cookie stuck in one side, and the chocolate casing had to be cracked to get at the ice cream and the cookie had to be broken out of the casing. It was fun to excavate the ice cream with the small metal spoon by stabbing, prying, and digging, but it became more work than fun so they pushed aside what was left and leaned back in the chairs, facing downhill, sipping the coffee, regarding the view of the old port and higher up and in the distance the gold dome of the church. Shards and tiny slivers of reflected sunlight on the hill might have been the tourist train. All was peaceful. The only place he could imagine as peaceful as this was back home at dusk, with Alex running across the lawn at fireflies with her arms out. There was a gentle peal of church bells. The sun was pleasantly hot on them in a clear sky, and a breeze lulled them. This was the Place de Lenche. Harv said they would remember this, and Bev said, Yes, yes we will.

Alex their granddaughter had been suspended from school for fighting. Suspended for two weeks. Alex hadn't started it. The other girl had hit Alex first. The other girl was to blame for all of that, really. Alex had made a return jab, a straight punch with her right hand, and she'd put her weight behind it. The two girls, who were able fighters, had tussled in the cafeteria until adults pulled them apart. The school had a rule: a student was not to hit a student back, but instead to immediately report it to a teacher. Students had been told: heel toe directly to a teacher. Harv and Bev agreed that a sentence of two weeks, this late in the school year, was harsh adjudication for defending oneself. Alex would do her schoolwork at home. Suspended! Lessons would be delivered to the house by the school. Another incident at school would mean expulsion.

Bev said Alex was young. Harv knew it wasn't age. Age isn't what Bev had meant. The girl didn't know anything of the world. For the child there were only two sides of the world, the inside cool and the outside not cool. The inside was with the cool kids. The outside was with no one. Either one was inside or one was nowhere at all. Not cool meant meaningless. It seemed impossible to explain to Alex otherwise.

Harv said he'd been thinking that they could not allow Alex to go on without seeing the world outside of Alabama. Most kids were like this, they agreed. Bev said she'd been thinking the same thing, and she'd think on it some more.

From the inner streets of the old quarter, a man approached. Harv had noticed him. The man had walked in front of a wall Harv had been looking at where someone had written, in spray-paint with big round letters, *misere populaire 13*. Harv did not understand what those words meant. Perhaps the man had thought that Harv was looking at him, because he walked up to their table.

The man had a thin face and a lean chin held high in the way a young man might, though Harv believed him to be in his thirties or possibly early forties. A leather satchel at the end of his left arm. Dressed well enough, like a salesman. The satchel might be full of insurance policies to sell. The man introduced himself as Benjamin Iles. This is what Harv understood him to say. Harv's instinct was to wave him away, as he might a Roma gypsy man asking him to buy a rose, because the guide books had set him on guard against the schemes of Roma gypsies. But he did not wave this man away. He didn't know what the man wanted from them. It was curious. It was a game; Harv was trying to get at what he wanted. The man seemed humble. It was because of the way he spoke with a hand on his chest. The man seemed a good, kind, and even generous type except for his eyes, the flat dark discs in his eyes.

The man Iles spoke of cathedrals. He was French, of this Harv felt certain, though his English was very good, accented in some way that wasn't American. Harv didn't know much about the way people spoke English in different places around the world.

Iles was saying that from the old port one is able to see the three cathedrals of Marseille. One can see the Notre-Dame de la Garde on its hill, the good mother as they call it. For very good reason they call it this, Iles told them. One can see it from everywhere in Marseille, this cathedral that has always watched over the city and the Marseillais. And in strolling the quays one sees the church Saint-

Ferréol les Augustins, its white façade visible from everywhere in the old port, situated as it was in the belly of the port on the Quai des Belges, just off the arterial Canebière. But this was not a cathedral, if one considered the difference between an église and a cathedral. The Église Saint-Ferréol les Augustins was not the third cathedral.

And Iles said that out along the quays, further out toward the mouth of the port, one can see the Cathedral de Saint-Marie-Majeure. This was the second cathedral. At the end of summer there would be a great procession from the cathedral through the streets of Le Panier with a golden statue of the Virgin. One might consider, then, that a cathedral was a point of departure on a scale that an église was not.

Iles stopped talking and Harv waited to hear about the third cathedral. Harv didn't want to have to ask for it. He thought he knew what the third cathedral was. It was the old church Réformés on the Canebière, on the way up to the Palais Longchamp. They hadn't walked that way yet, he hadn't seen it, but he'd read about it. He'd read there was a Joan of Arc statue up there. When the man didn't say anything else, Harv ventured, "The third one is the church Reforms."

"Which one? Ah, Réformés."

"That's the one."

"Les Réformés," Iles repeated, "l'église Saint-Vincent-de-Paul," looking briefly into the distance, into the middle of the Place de Lenche, as if measuring the truth of this answer. Iles said an argument could be made for this, it wasn't entirely absent of truth, but then there would be four cathedrals. With respect to those cathedrals one is able to see from the old port, there were only three.

Bev was squinting at Iles. For both of them, the sky was bright behind Iles. Bev said, "The Saint-Laurent church?" A pink stone church, very small and very old. They'd walked briefly through it, and there wasn't much to see. It was high up, near the mouth of the port, not far from where they were now. Harv mostly remembered the view of the port from in front of it.

Iles said Saint-Laurent was not the third cathedral.

The server passed nearby—a young woman, in a white apron, going among the empty tables to clear cups and bowls, piling these on her tray—and Harv said to her, "Excuse me, miss. La addish onion see-el vus play?" and she replied, "The check?" She said this without looking at him as she left with her tray of cups and bowls. Harv said to Iles, "Do we keep guessing?" He wasn't sure he wanted to continue the game. It seemed vaguely that the more time they spent with this man the more risk, whatever it was that was at risk.

Bev said cheerfully, "I'm sure I can guess. Let me have the map."

"If I tell you," said Iles, "then you will find it on your own. The cathedral on the hill is glorious, and this one on the north side is, too." He waved in the direction of the Cathedral de Saint-Marie-Majeure. "The third cathedral is like these. Some say it is the most glorious of the three." He placed his hand on his chest. "I say so. You will find it to be the most beautiful place you have ever visited. It is not to be missed. I will take you there. I will be your guide."

So that was it. Harv felt more comfortable with him, now that he'd revealed the game. Harv said, "What's your price?"

"I will take you there for nothing more than it costs to take the train touristique."

Harv glanced at Bev. She'd unfolded the map and was staring down at it. She was letting him handle this part of it. They'd seen a few churches today already. They had a plan. The museum would be next. Too many churches were depressing. They ought to mix them in. But if she wanted to visit another church he'd be a good sport and with the camera he'd shoot the hell out of it like he had the others. Without looking up, Bev said, "The train was not inexpensive. Maybe another time."

Harv said to her, "You're right about the train." He said to the man, "Thank you, monsieur, for the offer. But we'll pass." He'd wanted to say the man's name but wasn't confident that he had it right. He'd never heard the name Iles before. He wanted to call him Ben. Wouldn't that be easier? But he didn't want to offend him. They stood up because the server arrived with the bill and Harv gave her the euros and plenty extra for tip.

"Good day," the man said with a smile, and then said something in French, probably to have a good day, or to have a good holiday, or something along these lines that was neighborly. He walked away, the way he'd come, heading back into the depths of the old quarter.

Harv hung the camera on his shoulder, folded up the map properly, and looked one last time from there, the Place de Lenche, at the view of the port and of the gold-domed church up on its hill. The man was gone, and the server cleared the table from which Harv had walked only a step away. The server asked them what the man had wanted.

"He offered to take us to the third cathedral." It seemed that she had difficulty understanding his English. He went on to explain that this man Iles had said there was another cathedral and that he would lead them to it, for a price.

She squinted up at the sky briefly. She said, "I don't know it," and took away their cups and bowls.

He asked her, "Can I help you with that?" He carried some of the cups and bowls inside. Harv respected these port people. Because of his early years in the Navy, he felt connected to them. Because of all that he'd done in those days, he might even have a child in a port like this one. He could not know whether or not he had a child among them and he would never know. He hadn't been Harv back then. His fellow seamen had called him Harry. That Harry person didn't exist anymore. That Harry person had existed for only that brief time. Someone would never be able to track him down as a Navy man named Harry.

Before he left, he asked the server, who was about the age of their daughter, "Did you grow up here in Marseille?"

"Yes," she said, with a smile. "It's okay."

He and Bev had decided early on to have one child and that was what they'd done. Bev wasn't built for it. He'd nearly lost her during the birth of their daughter.

It was not far from there to the Museum Regards de Provence. Harv and Bev walked through the *Mediterranean Reflections* exhibition. Paintings of old Marseille and maritime scenes and Mediterranean ports. It was in front of a colorful painting by Émile-Othon Friesz, *The Calanque at Figuerolles, 1907,* when Harv said in a long sad exhale, "Look at how they see things," and by this he meant the painter's way of seeing and what painters do with color to put what they see on canvas, and then Bev held his arm and leaned on his shoulder, and he realized that she was crying. He hadn't expected it. What struck him was that she was hurt and in pain because her man was losing his eyes and there wasn't a thing she could do about it. Her emotion made him swell up with emotion, too. Had something triggered this? Had it been the man Iles, all that talk of a hidden cathedral? Harv had trouble speaking now with a thick of emotion in his throat but he managed to say, quietly, "None of that now. We promised none of that."

"You won't see Alex grow up."

"Like hell I won't."

He huffed. He was trying to use anger to tamp down the feelings. But it wasn't tamping them down, so they sat on a bench at the bottom of stairs that led up to the next floor of the exhibition until she stopped crying and he recovered, too.

After the museum Harv and Bev walked around the outer edge of Fort Saint-Jean and from over the stone walls watched boats come into the port from the sea. Some ferries, some sailboats. Bev said, "We just saw somebody's picture of that," as she pointed vaguely out at the scene. Plenty of other people were out on the walkway. A few were fisherman with lines in the water. Some others had climbed down onto the tumble of big mossy rocks at the water. Had the man Iles ruined the Place de Lenche for them? Where would Iles have led them? Harv and Bev continued on to the Quai du Port, the north side of the port, and took a table at the front edge of one of the many café terraces. Bev had a Perrier with a rondelle, which was a lemon slice on the rim of the glass. Harv had a Provençal rosé wine, something Coteaux d'Aix-en-Povence. They were asked to pay when served the drinks, accompanied by a bowl of mixed nuts. Her water was more expensive than his wine. They were resting. All was pleasant. Things were happening around them that were not especially unique to anywhere but nonetheless charmed them. The server was attending to other tables. People were passing by on the quay. A few on bicycles. A boat was up on a dry dock and someone was washing it. At piles of fishing nets, a man was untangling one, or repairing it, or simply tying lines. An old man stopped to ask if they wanted to buy cigarettes. He had a pack in his hand. Harv said no, not unkindly, and the old man then asked at the next table and the next.

Harv did not talk about the feelings they'd experienced at the museum. It was no use talking more and more about his disease. Tearful episodes had happened and he knew tearful episodes would happen again and again. Episodes would happen as unexpectedly as it had at the museum. That was just part of it. Part of life and part of sharing lives together. But they did talk more about Alex. When their daughter had been as young as Alex was now, they'd sensed something under the surface of her, something they could not put into words. They stared down at the marble café table's veins. It had been like these veins. Something they could see just beneath the surface of her, something of substance, something of her soul, they agreed. But they did not see this in Alex. They couldn't easily put it into words. The young were different today, they agreed. This was as close as they could get to it.

They opened the map on the table. Bev leaned over the map and ran her fingers across it saying the names of the churches. But there would not be another church today. Harv suggested taking the ferry out to L'Estaque, known as the painter's district, which the guidebook recommended. But it might be too late in the day to try to see all of L'Estaque. Tomorrow then, in the morning, they might take the ferry from the old port to that fishing village. The ferries, or *les navettes*, ran on the half hour all day between seven and seven. Famous painters like Cézanne and Renoir had lived and painted there. Harv had read that there was a path marked by plaques, all about the painters. Bev agreed the place would be something special to see. One could also take a navette to the Frioul islands and the Chateau d'If, the famous prison, its most famous prisoner the Count of Monte Cristo.

Harv spotted the man Benjamin Iles going by out on the Quai du Port. He pushed back his chair and rushed out, Bev behind him.

"Iles, look here, Iles," Harv said, catching up to him. Iles was the same, except Harv noticed worn brown leather shoes. The seams were shot. It didn't mean anything. "Monsore," Harv said. "Monsore Iles."

Iles stopped and turned, making a close arc with the brown satchel at the end of his arm. The satchel, too, was worn at the handle rivets and the stitching of its buckle straps. None of this meant a thing about the man.

"Hello," said Iles.

Harv was out of breath: "The Sacré Coeur. Over by the bus stops. It's the third, isn't it?"

Iles smiled broadly. "Ah, the Basilique du Sacré Coeur. No, monsieur. That one is not the third. The Sacré Coeur is far from here, far but not very far, on the avenue du Prado, beyond the Place Castellane. The Basilique du Sacré Coeur is beautiful. I have been there many times. How good of you to think of it. But the third. The third is greater than the Basilique du Sacré Coeur. The third is a cathedral."

"Look here, what's your game?" Harv got closer to him. "There is no third cathedral."

"I beg your pardon?"

"Just say it, Iles."

Bev cried, "Don't hit him!" She'd put herself between them. "He's sick, don't hit him, he's sick!" She was saying this to Iles, not the other way around.

Harv said, "Get out from the middle of us, Bev." Iles didn't look like a man about to throw a punch. Harv had rolled his hands into fists but didn't intend to start anything. He only wanted Iles to admit it was a sham. Harv hadn't hit a man in over thirty years. He just wanted the truth. He moved in close to Iles and growled, "None of this is for me, Iles. You understand? These shots are for my granddaughter and she's eleven and by God you mess that up and I'll rip your head off."

Bev cried, "Harv!"

Iles said, "I will take you to it."

"Yes you will," Harv said.

"For what I offered, the cost of two tickets on the train."

Harv unrolled euro notes as they began to follow him, while Iles walked ahead, while Iles said, "It is faster to go this way. Come this way." Harv caught up and handed him the euro notes. He and Bev followed him on streets and passages that led away from the old port.

Harv said, "It is not the Cathedral de Saint-Marie-Majeure? We're not far from where we were earlier. Isn't the water over there? I could be wrong. I don't really know where we are."

Iles said, "The oldest things, these are in the center." He stopped at a corner and said, "Have you seen this? It is the oldest house. See the old street names on the walls of the house. Those street names, they are not this street. This street has another name. The house was moved. Of course it is true also that some streets in Marseille have more than one name, so it is never clear where one is located, certainly not on a map such as the one you have." Iles was watching behind them. "Are we being followed?"

Harv looked back. There were people out walking on the streets. Nothing seemed different about it. "Who would be following?"

"Come this way, quickly," Iles led them across the street and along another passageway and out onto another street. He said to them, "If others know, they will want to see it."

"What is the name of it?"

"Back this way," he said, as the streets became shorter, the turns more abrupt, the passageways more narrow. "It's this way." And then they stepped out onto a wide street, crossed it, and again through passageways.

Harv said, "This way, Bev," because she was falling behind. "Here, it's this way." He waited for Bev while he kept a watch up ahead for Iles, and on occasion he saw Iles look back at him. He saw Iles turn, making a close arc with the brown satchel, and nod to him as if to say that he would pause, that he would walk slower. And there seemed only one way to go now, between buildings as they were, with narrow stone stairs and passageways. It must've been the old quarter, Le Panier.

Harv lost sight of Iles. "He's up ahead. He'll wait for us." When Harv and Bev left the passageway at the next wide street, Iles was not there.

Bev turned herself around. "Where is he?"

She was breathing hard, and so was he. "Bev, I think he's gone."

"No, it can't be."

There were cafés and shops, and other streets and passageways. It did not seem a place of tourists. The people walking by and milling about in the shops seemed of Marseille. Harv did not see Iles anywhere. They waited for him at the mouth of the passageway. Harv found a spot for Bev to sit on the ground with her back against a stone wall. He sat next to her.

They waited, but Iles did not come back.

3

Corey

Corey climbed the long road up the hill. There were countless ways up to the church, the highest point in Marseille, the Notre-Dame de la Garde. He hadn't expected this way on the road to be as exhausting as it was, the sun as hot. Others were making the same climb, but he did not see Samira among them. He hadn't walked this way since his first days in Marseille in early summer. The Marseillais called this church *la bonne mere*, the good mother, because it had always been there to watch over them. He was on his way to meet Samira.

There was clear aim and purpose to Corey's time in Marseille, in this summer of 2013. He'd come to research his doctoral dissertation, like Noémie. He'd been surprised to discover other doctoral students there, all from various universities. They all knew each other, though he felt closest to Noémie. Among them, he could not help but feel inferior, acutely out of place. Their passions were not his passions.

At twenty-four, he'd put an ocean between himself and all that had been home for him. He was well on his way, but he'd never felt so uncertain about the place in life he'd come to, as if his life trajectory had been an action of forces that he could not observe. All of this was a strange mix of anguish and thrill.

After the long road up the hill, there were high steps. Corey arrived breathing hard up the last few to, first, the crypt, and then to what was called the upper church. He wandered like an untethered tourist among the neat rows of pews under three high cupolas, red and white marble pilasters, and small wooden ships hovering in the air, suspended by string. These ship replicas were ex-votos, offerings of gratitude. This nave smelled of burning coal and incense. It smelled of men like priests and parishioners who conducted themselves according to values deemed acceptable. It smelled of the many. It did not smell of the few, like him, who felt apart, because he did not do what everyone expected of him. Tourists brushed past him. Some were impatient, because Corey had lingered too long. He was not one of them. He did not have a camera. He was looking at them. They were looking at the church.

Corey went out to the terrace and took in the views on all sides of Marseille and of the coast and out to sea. The distance was palpable. Tourists were shooting the view from every edge of the terrace. He did not know what they were seeing in the distance that was different than what he was seeing. He was further from home than they were.

He looked among them for Samira. In the middle of the night, he'd spoken to her on rue Saint-Savournin. They'd discussed possibilities, and she'd agreed to meet him here at the church.

Home for him had been his parents, their house, the New Jersey town. In that town, he'd passed his youth in two houses. One house before he was twelve and a second after. The houses had been about the same, not considerably far from one another, only the second had more rooms and more yard. But to Corey, the youngest of three boys, when the family had moved from one house to the other, they had moved worlds away, marking a fault line in him. It had changed him from the declarative mode of, *Today, this is who we are*, to the mode of *Where will we be, after today?* which was inquisitive and prying.

To his parents, a house was a house was a house, and what mattered was home, which came as a result of a job and a wife and children. A job would provide for the future. To Corey, a job was a job was a job. It was men who were nuanced and had differences, if one only took the time to notice. Nothing in life was as simple as his parents had led him to believe.

He found Samira, at last, waiting for him on a bench, purse on her lap. She might've only just arrived. He almost didn't recognize her. He sat next to her, and they each said hello in the other's language. Samira could speak very little English. Corey's French was better than her English but in this moment all words seemed awkward and inadequate. He gave her money. She quickly counted it and then put it in her purse. She scooted closer to him. She was wearing a perfume that he found neither tasteful nor distasteful. He did not mind the floral aroma of it, though he could not name it. He did not know the names of flowers in his mother's garden, though his mother had spoken of them countless times. He had trouble with the names, because a marigold was not gold. A blue spruce was not blue. Was it, or wasn't it? The labels were all wrong. Samira put the purse down on the other side of her. They watched the swooping mouettes. He observed, in French, that collisions do not happen in the sky. Samira said that they do, sometimes, when no one is looking.

Samira offered to do things. Samira knew this language well. It was universal. Corey wanted to but did not know what of his wants to act on. Samira asked what he'd like to do. She said there were things they could do at her apartment on rue Saint-Savournin that they both wanted. He did not lie to her. He described some of the things he'd been thinking about doing. She said that she could help him find his way to these things.

She made suggestions. She asked if he was interested in any of these suggestions. She offered to be his mother.

"No," he quickly said, not my mother.

Samira said, "I'm a good mother."

"I have absolute confidence that you are."

Samira asked, "Where is she?"

He wanted to tell her. He wanted to tell Samira everything. He told her that his mother rang him constantly to chat on video from New Jersey, at his computer on his desk in a clutter of books and papers. She was in her kitchen, with her laptop on the granite island. For him, everything behind her was where he was from, what had made him, and as familiar to him as his own skin. For her, everything behind him, in Marseille's La Plaine quarter, she could not see and would never know first-hand. She hadn't seen many foreign places. She'd never flown to Europe. She and his father had honeymooned in Niagara Falls. To experience somewhere else, she took the train into New York City. She'd been to foreign restaurants in midtown. To her it was as good as anywhere else could be. She was not interested in stepping off a plane in an unfamiliar place. As much as she worried about him, she was not going to visit him in Marseille. No one was going to visit him in Marseille. He didn't bother to pick up his clothes or make the bed. There would only be video chats.

Samira asked in French, "So you are alone?"

He said it was his mother who was alone. On screen, his mother wore yardwork clothes and had less time to tend to her tomato plants because there were no sons left at home to mow the grass, pull weeds, deadhead the roses. Sometimes she rang him with a spade in hand and stared at him like he was a problem plant. Something wasn't right with the youngest of the coneflowers. It was unsightly without its blooms. The leaves had curled—was it unhappy? Her coneflowers caused her such worry. Her friends had asters. Asters were easier to read. Her friends did not seem to have as much to worry about as she did.

His mother said that he should be back where he belongs. A transplant that wasn't doing well needed to be moved back. But none of this was what she was trying to say. She wanted him to work hard, like his brothers had. His brothers had done it right. She wanted him to have the home for himself that hard work promised. Until he was ready to do that, she preferred him under her care. She would prefer him swimming at the Spring Brook club pool and taking tennis lessons. Practicing his serve. Rubbing elbows with wives of city commuters, wives whose husbands were entrée and daughters were, respectably, prey. This was what young men did. And he was a normal young man! On the patio he would perfect how to cook dead things in the smoker. He'd work in the yard. Yard work was worthwhile hard work. It taught lessons for later in life, for work in the city. It was hard work that would take him to new places: a wife, children, and his own house in New Jersey. Hard work would lead to a midtown office, as it had for his brothers before him. If only he would work hard on things that mattered. She didn't understand his academic work, why studies were so important to him, and why he'd gone so far away. His aimless days would only lead him further away from her and New Jersey and the life that she'd raised him to lead. She was trying to say these things.

He'd told his mother on screen that all of our futures depended on a closer look at this gateway of cultures, this capitol of former colonies, this nerve center of North Africa.

Samira asked if he understood the French well enough. She said it was difficult to understand some of what he was saying.

He said that he understood better than he could speak. He'd studied the language for years, so he knew a lot of words and many of the common expressions.

She said that she knew every word in French but she did not have all the words to say what she wanted to say about his mother. She said in French, "Your mother understands you more than you know because everyone is not very different."

Corey told Samira that he'd mentioned her to his mother on screen today.

Samira asked, "Is it true?"

He told her all that they'd said on screen. His mother had wanted to know, Who was this friend Samira? Who was this woman friend, and what did she mean to him? She'd wanted the whole story. She had to dig for answers. Why wouldn't he tell her everything? He used to. All of it worried her. Corey made up things to tell her. He lied because she worried so much. He told her that he was safe because there was no crime in Marseille. She wanted to hear that he locked his door at night. It was true, he locked his door at night, but other things he said were not true. He described Marseille as a coastal town with plane trees and café terraces, on the Mediterranean's bluest water. Its wines were white and rosé. He'd told her, Everyone was so friendly. People smiled and said hello. They opened doors for you, offered to carry your bags.

Samira laughed as he said these things, and she wanted to know, "What else?"

He'd told his mother that he liked to walk the sandy beaches. The beaches were clean, and never crowded. He liked to watch the sailboats. On the weekends he might take up sailing. The waters were always calm. Boats let other boats pass. They lowered their sails. No boat was in a hurry. Everyone had plenty. Because she worried, he told his mother these things that were so far from the truth. He did not mention the poverty, the sprawl, the tower blocks of the suburbs, the drug trade, the automatic weapons flowing in from the Balkans and North Africa. Instead he told her that everyone was under plenty of sun. Was he eating enough? Yes, he told her, there was food everywhere and in fact no one in Marseille went hungry. The light, he said, was crystal clear. The colors were vivid. Painters came from all over the world. Plein air painting was the most popular sport in Marseille. Wasn't it too hot there? Yes, the sun was hot but he didn't mind. It was quiet at night. It was like sleeping in a cloud and every morning he was refreshed. Yes, his apartment had a washer and dryer, and there was always hot water. He lied in all of these ways, but still she worried.

It was clear to him that his mother didn't understand why he told her the things that he did. He talked about the couscous at the blue-tiled La Kahena off the vieux port. She said that couscous was couscous was couscous. She wouldn't say it but it was clear that she knew he wasn't telling her the things that mattered. Her look on screen seemed to say, *Something is wrong with my son.* She wanted to know, What did it mean when he talked about practicing his petanque *tirer au fer*? She wasn't familiar with petanque. She didn't know the rules. She didn't care to know, but she wanted to understand why it meant so much to him.

While Corey and Samira spoke, from time to time a passerby noticed that Samira was not a she. Only once did someone, an older French woman, say something loud enough to be heard. Corey in a swell of anger stood up to reprove the woman, but Samira pulled him back down to the bench with surprising strength, held his arm, and said to him, "Let's keep having fun," which must have been words that she used at other times with her customers.

Samira asked, "And your father?"

Corey said that he did not have much to say about his father. His father rang in the evenings to chat on video. He took the Morris & Essex line in from Penn Station. All day, he suffered the whining of CEOs, some as young as his three sons. He worked with CEOs to pull apart what they'd built and put it back together under other media companies. It must have been exhausting because at home he had nothing left for his family.

Corey's friend Chuck from all the way back to middle school had suggested that he was working hard not to be his father. Nothing was more obvious, Chuck had told him, and anybody could see it. Corey would do anything to become a man other than his father. Which didn't make any sense, Chuck had said, because his father was an okay guy, a regular suit and tie, a regular briefcase and commute into the city. His father was all right. There wasn't a closet full of weirdness. His father wasn't doing anything wrong. Chuck had asked him, "Is that what you want, Corey, to be a little bit wrong?"

"Maybe it was," Corey said.

Samira agreed, Maybe it was.

Corey was not familiar with all of the rude French words the old woman had used. He asked Samira but Samira would not repeat the words. Samira said they were vulgar words. Samira asked where Chuck was and why he wasn't with him.

He wanted to tell Samira everything. He told her there were many pockets of things. He told her that Chuck rang on screen from time to time. When he did, Corey put down the Walter Benjamin he'd been reading, while Chuck opened a matchbook to light the cigar that looked on screen way too big for his face. Chuck chewed gum at the same time. Everything was easy for Chuck.

Chuck had said, "Dude, young men like us need girls by the handful."

Chuck told him that he'd hook him up with his cousin's friend, a real looker, who happened to be in Nice, though Chuck didn't realize how impossibly far away Nice was, in every way. He had girls in town who wanted to meet Corey. He said these girls by the handful. He said they'd double-date to get Corey back in action.

Corey told him that this word double-date wasn't unlike *la double peine* in Marseille: if you were an undocumented immigrant and you were caught doing a crime, then you had to do both the time and also you were deported. This was *la double peine*.

To this Chuck said that Corey could only hope to be caught *in flagrante delicto* while on a date with a Nice girl. It was one of the great achievements available to men. Chuck held up the cigar and said, "You will wear it like a badge."

Corey explained that after expulsion, one would have to find a way back. This was the way of *la double peine*. There in Marseille, there were undoubtedly ways. Anything could be bought, traded, or sold.

Samira asked him to slow down because it was difficult to understand.

Corey told her what Chuck had said, that there were young things filling out just for him. Chuck said he'd seen them on upper Speedwell and on Pine Street by the library, just waiting for him to come back from France. Chuck repeated Speedwell and Pine Street. Chuck said that repeating the street names would help keep the town in Corey's recent memory because Corey was trying to leave it behind. Chuck had seen some really hot things at Burnham Park. He repeated Burnham Park. He said he'd never thought to look there for girls, neither of them had.

Samira said, "Your mother knows my name now. She tells your father. She tells Chuck. She tells everyone. Is it okay?"

Corey said that he'd tried to tell Chuck things. But it was difficult to explain what no one wanted to hear. When he'd told Chuck that he'd talked to a prostitute, the ones on rue Curiol, Chuck had exclaimed brightly, "Dude!" Corey tried to explain to him but it was difficult so instead he explained that some of the prostitutes didn't speak English but they didn't need to. They didn't need to explain who they were to anyone, and he envied them for that. Corey knew Chuck would ask for a picture of one. When Corey sent the picture to him on-screen, Corey waited for the reaction. Chuck's eyes widened, and then Chuck said, "Dude, is that a—?"

Corey told Chuck he couldn't tell anyone what he'd done with fifty euros. Not anyone. Corey said if it got back to his parents he'd murder Chuck with a blunt instrument. He waved the heavy Walter Benjamin book at the screen. Chuck said, "I get it," and sat back in his chair further away on screen, with his eyes still wide.

Chuck then said he needed to process and ended the call, but not before Corey told him again not to tell anyone, the thing to tell people was that he was seeing things that he could not back home, he was visiting the North African market streets, he was getting to see paintings in the Museum Regards de Provence, he was experiencing the cathedral the old port the Chateau the Abbey the sea—Chuck hung up on him.

Samira said, "He is not here for you. I am. They are not with you. I am."

"I have absolute confidence."

"What does this mean?"

"It means I understand that you will be on rue Saint-Savournin."

"Yes," Samira said. "Come see me again. I will always be there. Let's keep having fun."

4

Evie

It was George who pulled Evie off the low wall of the Cours Julien square and made her drink with him and his friends, three Americans, between band sets at the Pussy Twisters bar on rue Crudère, not far from his apartment on rue Carnot. It was a fifties night, but not. It was a punk band with a playlist of fifties covers. A band from nearby Aubagne, with guitars and drums, sickly thin youths, amped wailing that one might recognize as the sounds of Elvis Presley, Johnny Mathis, Bill Haley, Bobby Darin. Pussy Twisters was so small, a half dozen standing to listen were enough to crowd the room, and if no one showed, always the band members could pull a few dead end street kids from the wall of the square. The others in the bar were a few friends of the band in similar awful shape, or worse, drug dealers on the scent of these types.

His friends weren't as keen, but George wanted Evie to talk, to get her straightened out. She smelled of the street. Her cheeks were ruddy, her nose and chin red. Someone had put her hair in dreads. Her hands were an older woman's. She was twenty-three. What was wrong with her? It was booze. Word had gone around that she'd been raped by men from all over these Cours Julien streets; she'd get so drunk with a man that she couldn't stop him. And so it became her reputation, and it kept happening.

She'd come up two years ago from Cape Town with a boyfriend, but then he'd left her behind, he'd moved on to another gig in Germany. What prick would leave a girl behind in this place? She'd ended up on the wall of the Cours Julien square.

George didn't want her to down so many whiskey drinks but it was helping her talk about it. Her South African English came off proper, girlish, and sweet. She swayed when she spoke. She said she'd been on the streets with Bernard. "Who?" George wanted to know. "Oh!" George laughed at the use of the guy's full name, a homeless punk on the wall, because everyone called him Burner. It had stuck. George said it was ridiculous, no one was with Burner. He was one of those out for himself. She said he'd been good to her. George felt it was no use to go at Burner's character. He wasn't anything real to her.

At one point while they were speaking English she called him Bernie, and he said, "No, don't confuse us, I'm George."

She said brightly, "Well of course you are!"

George asked if she was getting high besides the booze and she said she didn't have money to do that.

She said her family used to send money but they'd stopped when they learned she went to the clinic and got rid of—

George made her stop there. He didn't want to hear about her family.

She said anyway there was some money left in South Africa. She said Nicolas gives her a hard-boiled egg some mornings. George knew him, the owner of Le Même, a café on the square. She splits the egg with friends. George asked her if it was really one egg, and she said, "That's all I need. Of course the bakery gives us old bread and we get them weed." She laughed: "Bakers *love* weed."

George asked, "Who's we?"

She shrugged: "All of us."

"What if you're caught?"

She admitted she had no papers and he saw the glint of fearful apprehension in her eyes that he'd seen among the undocumented in Marseille. He thought that's when she was going to really go at the core of all that was going on with her but then she said she had a lead on a job to be a school teacher. He said, "But you're undocumented." She said it was a good lead from a Greek she'd met on rue Saint Ferréol. She explained it was to tutor English and she wouldn't need papers for that. George threatened to take away her drink to shut her up because all of that wasn't real, he didn't want to hear her delusions.

She said she'd even found a good spot, one of the stone benches out on the square where she could tutor someone's cub if only she could get some pencils and paper.

"Show me where," George said, and he pulled her out of the bar. They went through the square and she held onto his arm, drunk out of her mind, both of them were. From the wall the dead end street kids, the drifters, and the drug dealers heckled her so George turned her onto rue Carnot. He said, "In the shape you're in you need to stay at my place." She didn't say no so he took her up to his apartment.

5

Corey

Corey went to the party that everyone talked about. This party happened every year at a certain address in Marseille's Noailles quarter. Corey didn't have an invitation and didn't know the host. He didn't know if the host was a man or a woman. The party was on such a scale, it was probably more than one person. The party, as everyone knew, filled to bursting. It was at a sprawling but plain apartment with rooms up and down stairs. Some said the apartment was a cube, as many stories high as it had rooms on each floor. But no one knew the layout well. There was no one to ask. No one worked the door, and no one seemed to be in charge.

He didn't need an invitation. No one needed an invitation. Of those who went to wild parties at night, everyone went to this party. Certainly all the students went. Certainly all the American students who'd found themselves to be in Marseille.

Everyone knew that the party could be dangerous. Always it was overcrowded and loud. Lots of people were drunk, and some were rough when they were drunk. Corey saw a Senegalese man hit another Senegalese on the head with an aluminum baseball bat. The blow knocked the man to the ground.

By this time Corey was wine drunk. What occurred to him was the question, Where did this man get a baseball bat? He said it in French to a young woman who happened to be beside him in the crowd, her hair in dreads. It looked to be a professional aluminum baseball bat. Baseball was not played in Marseille. No stores in Marseille sold an American baseball bat. The young woman asked, "Is it a cricket bat?"

Corey replied, "No, I know what a cricket bat is."

"Is it flat?"

"An American baseball bat is not flat. You must've seen one in the movies. It's a big round stick."

"Is he bleeding?"

She asked this in French but she could speak English. It was evident to him in the way of her French. But he could not know where she was from and did not ask. He was more interested in the baseball bat. Corey said, "Of course he's bleeding, because he was hit on the head with a baseball bat."

She asked in French, "What did he do to get hit?" This wasn't exactly the question she'd asked. It was a complicated question because there was something in the subtext of her words about deserving the blow, or asking for the blow, something about an inevitable consequence of one's actions, and Corey at first had some trouble understanding what it was that she was asking. He reduced it to, "Why had the one man hit the other man?"

Corey didn't know why the Senegalese man had hit the other Senegalese on the head. In the instant before it had happened, the bat had been raised in the air. The crowd had sensed this signal, and had shifted so that enough space was cleared for the one to swing the bat. This was when Corey had looked over and seen the blow. Such a blow to the head with a baseball bat might've killed the man. It did not, but he was bleeding badly. Corey did not think the injured man would get up, but it wasn't long before he did. The other Senegalese with the baseball bat was lost in the crowd, or in another room, or he'd left. The crowd filled the space where it had happened, and no one any longer seemed aware of what had happened or the bleeding man struggling to get to his feet or the blood on the floor. It might not have been blood. It might've been a spilled drink, but it was on the floor where the Senegalese had been lying. And it seemed to Corey there would be a lot of blood after such a blow to the head.

The bleeding Senegalese went from person to person blearily, very drunk it seemed to Corey. The Senegalese was asking each person if he could make a call on a cell phone. The first man in the crowd would let him use his cell phone. The next woman in the crowd would not, either. Another man would not, and another. The young woman with her hair in dreads would not. The young woman, with a lingering look at Corey, which he could not interpret, then moved away and was lost in the crowd. Corey had not had an opportunity to tell her that he was not without friends, that he'd found some people he knew at this party but hadn't found the someone he was looking for, and this was why he'd seemed to be alone, but he wasn't alone really. He was and he wasn't.

The bleeding Senegalese next asked Corey if he could borrow his phone. "I need to call for help," he said. The man was trembling. The man swallowed, waiting for an answer. His hands were wet with blood because he'd been touching his head. He was asking politely in French, and desperately. Corey asked him why no one was letting him use a phone. The Senegalese said it was because he was bleeding. He would get blood on the phone. Because there was so much blood.

Corey said, Well that's not a problem for me. He pulled his red cell phone out of his pocket and handed it to the man.

After the phone call and returning the phone the Senegalese man put his back against the wall, and slid down to sit on the ground, leaving a smear of blood on the wall.

"You're still bleeding," Corey said. "Is there something I can do?"

The man said it would be all right because they were coming for him.

"Who is coming for you?"

"Some friends."

"What is your name?"

"Abdou from Senegal."

Corey, as drunk as he was, asked if the other man was going to come back to hit him again, and Abdou said he did not know. Corey asked where the other man had bought the bat in Marseille, because there were no stores in Marseille that sold an American baseball bat. Abdou said he didn't know. Corey asked if it still hurt, and Abdou said, "Yes."

Corey asked if there was something that could be done for the bleeding.

"Leave it alone," Abdou said, but it was difficult for Corey to hear and understand Abdou's French in this loud room, with so many people. Abdou might've asked to be left alone.

Corey asked Abdou what he thought of the plans for the grand mosque north of the old port, and to this Abdou stared at him with no answer. Corey sat down next to him and explained that he was in the research phase of a doctoral program, that he was from New Jersey, which is in the United States, and that such topics were relevant or they were not entirely relevant to the broader subject of his work but at least were of interest to him and informed everything that he was doing. He asked Abdou if he was Muslim, and Abdou said, "Yes." Corey admitted that he had not done enough research on this topic, that there were academic papers to read, but at this early stage he understood from the newspapers that the Muslims did not necessarily need or want the grand mosque. Abdou said nothing. He'd closed his eyes. Corey wasn't sure if Abdou was still conscious, but in the next moment the eyes opened. He asked Abdou if his friends would be able to find him in this crowd. Abdou looked around at the people and did not answer.

Corey asked Abdou if he had family in Marseille, because for what other reasons do immigrants come to Marseille? Of course there could be many different reasons. Corey went on to say that he himself was not an immigrant and could not experience the reasons for himself but it was of interest to him. Probably the common language made it easier for immigrants to come from a place like Senegal, and from so many other places. Probably to immigrants the French-speaking world was like a miniature world that existed in effect on a plane between the whole world and the lines that governments draw between one another. It was like a set of states that were united by a common something that in this case was as simple as language, given a history of settlements, colonies, and the violence and brutalities that accompany these expansions. It was not unlike the United States.

Abdou said for work. "I came for work."

Corey asked about the journey from Senegal to Marseille, what must have been a grand and difficult journey. He didn't know the French word for arduous, so he said grand and difficult. Had there been a convoy of trucks, the kind where people sit in the back under canvas? Corey asked these questions. Had there been trouble along the way? There would be danger. Besides hunger and illness, there would be highway robbers. At the borders, what was it like to cross into another African country? Had some of the route required a camel? It must have been a grand journey all the way to Algiers and then the ferry across the Mediterranean Sea to here, to Marseille, at last.

Abdou said he had flown from Senegal. "That was all."

He asked Abdou if he was a secular Muslim. Abdou didn't seem to understand the question. Corey said that his French was not perfect because he'd first learned French conversationally, and so sometimes his French failed him. He asked Abdou if in his religion he was allowed to be as drunk as he was. Was he allowed to drink wine? What about beer? Abdou said he had not been drinking. Corey could not know if this was true. He asked again and Abdou had the same answer.

And then he asked Abdou if he prayed five times each day. Abdou said, "Yes." Corey asked him where he prayed, and Abdou explained that he prayed wherever he could. Often he prayed at a mosque that had been set up in the back of a shop in this quarter, the Noailles quarter. He named a street but Corey was not familiar with it. Abdou said that sometimes when he was elsewhere in the city, where there was no place to pray, he prayed on the street.

Corey opened his thin spiral notebook, the kind of notebook that journalists carry. He took the notebook everywhere he went in Marseille for occasions like this when he could jot down notes, and with his Pilot pen he wrote the name Abdou and what Abdou had told him about places of prayer.

Abdou's eyes were wide. He looked terrified. He exclaimed, "Are you police?" Corey said no, he was not police, he was a student. Abdou asked if police were coming. Abdou said that he knew nothing about any of his brothers and that nothing had happened here.

And then Abdou would not talk to Corey any more. Instead he watched the crowd in the room while wondering aloud to himself, quietly, so quietly that Corey had to lean in closer to hear and understand him: "Where are my friends? Where are my friends?" This question again and again.

Corey hit redial on his cell phone and when a man answered, Corey said in French, "What's taking you so long? Your friend is hurt. You must come. You must help him."

The phone was not part of him. He didn't care for it. It seemed in this moment to belong less to him than it ever had. He opened Abdou's hand still wet with blood and put the phone there.

"They're almost here," Corey reassured him, and then Corey stood up and left the room to find the young woman with her hair in dreads. He went downstairs, up other stairs, and further down found her in another crowded room. He was thrilled to have found her. Something inside of him swelled with elation. But she didn't seem to recognize him. He was confused. It was clear that she didn't recognize him. The swell inside of him broke, collapsed. He explained that it had only been moments ago when something had passed between them. She said she didn't understand what he meant. But a smile seemed to play on her lips that gave him confidence enough to go on. He explained that the man would be all right. He did not know whether to go back to the man or to stay with her. She asked, "Who?"

Corey said when he'd left the man, at least when he'd left him the man was all right, and friends were coming to get him, the man's friends. At least that's what the man had said to him. She didn't seem to know what he was talking about, so Corey had to start earlier, and he explained that the man was hit on the head with an American baseball bat. "You remember it, yes?"

She was shaking her head but he was thinking that yes, she must remember it. How could she not?

Corey had had too much to drink. He felt full. So all that he'd had to drink was still sinking into his system. He was dizzier than only a short while ago. A short while from now, he would be more drunk. The more drunk he was, the more his French failed him. It had always been this way.

While he was explaining what had happened earlier the young woman often looked away at the crowd. He stopped trying to explain things and asked her, "Are you alone?"

She said brightly, "Of course not!"

He said he was Corey, and she said she was Evie. He didn't know when they had switched to English but they had. Her accent was mysterious to him. He did not recognize it. She was not French, at least not from this part of France. He didn't ask where she was from because she would probably say a place that he knew nothing about. He knew very little about places other than where he was from and this foreign port, of which he'd learned more from words on paper than he'd experienced. He didn't want to talk about other places. He was afraid that it would become clear to her that he didn't know much of the world. She was not his type anyway. Chuck would have seen straight away that Evie was not his type. His friend Noémie would've seen it, too. Noémie would say, "This one? She's not for you." But none of his friends were there to tell him that Evie was not for him. He felt that he should go back to the injured man but he did not. He told Evie that the past is nothing, none of what happened with the man and the American baseball bat would be remembered tomorrow: it's our own struggle, isn't it, to figure out what's worth memory, here in Marseille, a port like this, a party like this, thrown together, aren't we, it's a great party but there are so many people crowded together that I don't feel like I'm here, if you know what I mean. We have where we are from and that's all we have. Who knows what's in store for us? A year from now. It seems an eternity away. A year and another year are eternities away but there's an urgency—don't you feel it? He asked again, "Don't you feel it?"

She lifted her shoulders and shook her head.

Corey said, "I feel the urgency."

She asked, "What do you feel? Are you angry? I don't get it. I'm sorry."

"Angry? I'm, I'm passionate, that's all. It's not the right word but here, here where we are, it's all I can come up with. Listen, the thing to remember is that we are here."

She asked, "You are saying you want to go to your place?"

"No, no, that's not what I mean. I mean yes, I wouldn't mind."

A group of people reached out for her, having recognized her. Evie in the next instant, just as quickly as she'd arrived in his life in Marseille, Evie bounced away, vanishing among the bodies of her friends.

Corey left the room, looking back for Evie though he could no longer see her in the crowd, and then he expected to find Abdou somewhere but he could not find Abdou among the rooms. Corey went downstairs, up other stairs, and through crowded rooms, pushing his way because he felt an urgent need to get to where he was going, though he had no idea where he needed to be. He was too drunk to think clearly. And then he wanted out. None of these rooms were familiar. None of the doors seemed to lead out. As he pushed through the crowd, he began to cry. It surprised him. He felt that a lesser man would cry. He wiped his eyes, lifting his hand. His arm caused someone's drink to spill but the crowd was so dense that none of this mattered.

The crowd seemed to swell and carry him, and then he was thrust out onto the street where there were many people whom he did not know but he was, at last, out of it and on his own again.

Shaken from the experience, he walked. He was walking it off, like an outfielder who'd dropped the baseball and lost the game for the team. He found himself on rue Saint-Savournin. He said hello to Samira. They each said hello in the other's language. He asked Samira if she was busy, if she was occupied. She said she was not, it was a quiet night, and everyone was hooking up at a big party. He gave her money. She quickly counted it, and led him upstairs.

Corey told her that he was drunk.

Samira asked, "What kind of drunk are you? A sad drunk?"

Corey said, "The first time I saw you, it was weeks ago, at night, I don't know what night it was or where I was heading. You were in the chair on the sidewalk. You said hello and I said hello. I remember that your hello was kind and generous. I smiled because when you said hello it pleased me to hear you, and you saw me smile, but I would not stop and talk to you. In effect, I refused to stop. I kept walking. My feet carried me. It's like my feet didn't belong to me. Part of me wanted to stop and talk to you, but the part of me was not my feet. I knew I could not, and so I walked away. I looked back at you, that was all. You called after me, again and again. I felt terrible."

Samira said, "You came again."

"I had to," Corey said. "I wanted to. I couldn't stop thinking about how I walked away from you. It was so unkind of me to walk away from you. You might be the one I have been hoping to find."

Samira put her arms around him and said, "Yes, you are drunk."

"When do we stop? And where, with what?"

"I will tell you."

Corey asked for her real name.

She said that she can have any name that he preferred. Her name had been Samira for a few years. Samira had been good for business. Customers preferred an exotic name.

6

Russ

There was not much at stake for Russ Bower, or so he believed. He had very few things left that were dear to him, and none of these were in Marseille, or in France, or overseas anywhere. Though his business was to expect the unexpected, he didn't expect this to change.

Russ was thirty-seven today. He had a rare non-pigmented melanoma cancer in him. He'd been told that he was near the end of his life.

&

At the hotel on the old port Russ took tea at two every afternoon, out on the terrace, and today there was a Roma gypsy girl he'd never seen before selling bars of soap from a cloth sack, and the usual older white-haired gentleman selling Lucky cigarettes, and the wind off the water, all of these going from table to table. And the lingering thugs and sailors, the long line at the ferry that may or may not arrive from Algiers, all of these usual things. A political march on the Canebière that was then beaten into pieces with batons. A fisherman throwing gaping dead sea things into the water, another one untangling a net. Always the untangling and tying of lines and nets because it was an everyday Tuesday at two in Marseille, and Russ sat in a chair built for him and his kind, who were tourists, or travelers, who were those drifting to see, to choose what not to see, to choose what not to see of themselves, at a café on the old port that existed for the very purpose of this, his tea at two, and this moment of—a fierce brawl interrupted his reverie, it was two men on the quay, and when the police arrived they beat the two and then left them on the ground rolling like spilled fish. Russ closed his eyes but it was not what he was supposed to do because when he closed his eyes in moments like this he saw the photos again. The photos!

He snapped his eyes open when a girl of eleven flitted out of the hotel, singing in French as easily as if she'd spoken it all of her little life, and then her mother banged out—"Rubbish," she was saying—with the hobo bag and a camera around her neck, and with a British sigh, a scowl. With the thugs and sailors taking notice, for they noticed everything, she informed Russ that she and her daughter were off to see the Cathedral on the north side of the port, and that he was welcome to join—yesterday she'd invited him to somewhere else—there was time enough left in the day, she said—but he chose to stay behind. Politely, he declined. "As you like," she said, and "another time." It always surprised him that others at the hotel said hello and invited him to join them, when he sat alone and did not invite them to speak to him. He was alone, for good reason.

He closed his eyes and there was winter sunlight on a stand of pines behind Ashley in Alabama, patches of snow on a scrubby stretch of field to the trees, but just now he'd rather not see the photos when he closed his eyes, as things had become what they had. Ashley was wearing a white scarf, a blue dress, boots, and her long hair tied up. The ease with which she tied up her hair in certain moments could change everything, like it had on their first night together while out walking, leaving Denver's Cheesman Park, walking on streets of old houses in the direction of the mountains in the sky where daylight was failing them, where uncertainty was ahead, except, when she tied up her hair as if to say she was comfortable with him, her white scarf loosened enough so that he touched her neck, it was instinct to touch her neck the affectionate way that he had, and it had changed everything. They had pulled each other closer and kissed.

In the photos that he saw behind his closed eyes he could not see all that she had done in Alabama. It was supposed to have been only a place where she had some friends. It was only where she'd gone to high school. Once or twice every year she flew over to Alabama. She flew from Denver to Birmingham, rented a car, and drove around, visiting friends. That was the extent of her Alabama. The sunlight on the stand of pines was on her, too, casting a shadow. She was alone in this photo. But her shadow was not alone. A man's shadow lay beside hers. And then for the next photo the camera had moved out and she and that man were crossing a field.

Russ did not know Alabama. He knew many places in many countries. He knew many dangerous places, because of his work, but he'd never been through Alabama. Of course a place was its people, and he found people to be generally the same everywhere. He worried a lot about this because he'd seen people do terrible things, one of the reasons he'd sent a man to watch her. He'd wanted to keep her safe. While she was away, he'd bought an engagement ring.

The next photo was in a bar: Ashley at a table with three women whom Russ did not know, and tall glasses of beer on coasters. Russ was trying to figure out what Ashley was saying to them. He thought through a thing before he said it, but she'd never been this way. Probably in this captured moment she was telling them that back in Denver she was dating a man who had cancer. Maybe a word like short-lived had slipped out of her mouth. It wasn't hard to imagine. There were empty chairs at the table, and no other men in this shot. It was not a snapshot. It had been taken by the watcher he'd sent. It was evident that the watcher had carefully composed this shot. His watcher had been an unseen observer, alone at a table across the room from them, probably a booth, because a booth provided cover, with the camera on the table casually. It would seem only coincidence that the camera was pointing in the direction of those four women.

In the next photo, on the other side of a grid of window panes, Ashley was on top of a man and they were both naked.

The analytical part of Russ's head was trying to keep the pain down in a box inside of himself and figure out where the two of them were, was it the same man as earlier, where were their clothes, was there a condom, but the rest of Russ, feeling bullied and hurt by the analytical part of him, didn't care a thing about any of these. All that mattered was that this had changed everything. He'd returned the ring to the jewelry store. He couldn't get all of his money back due to return fees and this had made him angry but he wasn't angry about the money. He mailed the photos to her. He didn't wait to hear back. He secured the windows of the house, the garden shed, and the back gate. And then he'd packed up and left. It was only to make a clean break from her, the analytical part of his head was saying, but there was fear mixed up in his feelings, a fear that he would give her another chance.

ॐ

Russ followed an old Marseillais man through the harbor. Russ imagined what the rumpled man was thinking: the man gazed with what seemed to be both wonder and surprise, during this late day stroll through the harbor, with an old woman at his side who was a wife or partner, with thin clouds blowing in the sky that at times took the sear out of the sun's heat, as this rumpled man gazed out from the water's edge at the Quai de la Fraternité at not the water, not at the water which does not change—the water only rises and falls—and not at the wind in the harbor, which the man could see because he'd worked on boats, he was a sailor—the wind does not change, the wind only blows and gusts, and it swells and swirls, and it whispers—but instead this man regarded the fishing boats and sailboats and ferries and the swooping mouettes, and also the café terraces, hotel fronts, souvenir shops, and the people who'd come to see all of it.

So much had changed—this was the man's wonder and surprise. The man had expected everything about the old port to change, but not so much of everything. Things had changed much more than expected. It felt like betrayal but it wasn't betrayal. The port had not made promises to him. The port had not made a vow. It wasn't betrayal. It was simply what was to be expected because this was Marseille, a city not like any other city. Marseille could be like the wind out on the sea. It could whip like the wind. It could fall quiet. Wind was wind and so it was not accurate to suggest that wind could change into something other than itself, but certainly wind could behave differently when least expected, which is why one must always watch the wind. This was what Russ believed that the man was thinking.

Following closely this old Marseillais couple around to the Quai du Port, the north side, Russ believed this about the man as much as he believed that his own left arm, with its metastatic melanoma, would be the death of him. Russ knew that he would leave this place with half as much understanding and wisdom as this old Marseillais. So Russ had immense respect for this man. Why did he have so much respect for a man he knew nothing about, a man from a different place, of a different language, a different culture, a different everything entirely?

Russ hadn't been a sailor. He couldn't see the wind. An American, from the Colorado plains, Russ was not built like the old Marseillais. He couldn't watch the wind. He couldn't look out at the sea and understand its currents. Russ envied the man—his look of wonder and surprise—what a gift it would be! To live to that age, to stroll through the harbor, this harbor of one's youth, where so much had changed. Did the old man recognize the hill over the old port? But of course, yes, one would always know the hill and its church the Notre-Dame de la Garde. A constant, a compass needle, a navigation point. A star in the night sky. Wasn't it, too, like the sight post on a rifle? The Marseillais called this church *la bonne mère*, the good mother, because she'd watched over them for centuries, and would not the Marseillais always call her the good mother, even when one day everything else has changed? The timeline of this good mother: in the thirteenth century, it was a chapel to the Virgin

Mary, and then a priory, and then a fort put up against the Romans, and so on, and so on. The timeline of his cancer: a shave biopsy by a Denver Medical dermatologist, and then a surgery at the hospital to excise the cancer, and then another surgery to excise it, and then other surgeries until the margins of the excision were found to be clear of melanocytes. But then the unexpected: learning that the lab work had been wrong, the facts were wrong, the margins had not been clear. There had been a mixup at the lab. Someone had made a mistake. Which never happens at a lab, they said, though it had. It was unheard of. Such a mixup never happens. The margins were not clear, even though an area as wide as a softball had been taken from his arm. The cancer had gone down inside of him. They could not know to where else. But they knew it had spread and they weren't able to cut it out, not all of it. He was nearer the end of his life than expected. Ashley, in her way that was funny, had said, "You're as good as dead." And then, "But we all are." She wasn't being mean. She was just going at the truth.

It was Ashley who'd begun to talk about the other patient, the one at the other end of the lab mixup. Now certainly that was a man incredibly relieved. The man's name would be Abe or Alan or Andrew. He and Ashley agreed that Abe Alan Andrew had started chemotherapy and had begun to think about all that he wanted to do before his end of days. This Abe Alan Andrew would have a wife and kids, wouldn't he? Yes, Abe Alan Andrew's house would be filled with the sound of children. Birthday parties with candles on cake and paper hats. But the mood had changed, since Abe Alan Andrew had been told that he had very little time left. It had to be explained to the children that their father would soon be leaving them. His wife would be inconsolable, but there wasn't time for that, because plans had to be made. Final arrangements were discussed. He wanted his ashes dumped somewhere in the mountains. His wife did not. She wanted their children and their children's children to have a gravestone to visit as they grew older. She asked, And what about me, if you're not beside me? And then the unexpected: Abe Alan Andrew received the good news: there'd been a mixup, he'd received the wrong end of the results, the margins of his excision were clear, he was after all going to make it out of this alive. His wife, his children, and all of his loved ones celebrated, threw a big party, invited everyone over. How did they describe what had happened? A cancer scare. A miracle. Did Abe Alan Andrew believe in miracles? Were they churchgoers? Abe Alan Andrew had narrowly escaped death. Death had had Abe Alan Andrew in its grasp, he'd grappled with death, he'd come out on top, and now would better himself. Probably all this was how it had been for Abe Alan Andrew, he and Ashley had agreed.

Russ, with hands out of his pockets now, followed the old Marseillais and the woman. The woman, this old Marseillais woman, had been the man's wife of many many years. Russ felt certain that they had children. He didn't know what had led him to this conclusion, but he felt certain about it. They had family, loved ones. They had health. Russ stood next to them further up on the Quai du Port and gazed with them at the old side of the harbor and up at the church. Boats with MARSEILLE lettered on one side, starboard, and sometimes one could read the name of the boat, almost always a name like CLAIRE, AIMÉE, or ÉMILIE.

Names a nurse might have. A nurse named Claire. A nurse named Émilie. A woman who talked to you during chemotherapy and you revealed things you would not normally reveal to a stranger and you felt that she did this, too. Names on boats. Russ had been on plenty of boats but preferred not to. He didn't have a lot of faith in them in the way he didn't have a lot of faith in elevators, or the rope bridges he'd once crossed while on special assignment in Ecuador. Usually in such situations as Ecuador he was forced to rely on such things as rope bridges. This was simply the way of the work that he'd been there to do. The chemotherapy, too, was a rope bridge. It was something one could not have a lot of faith in.

The old man had once been a fisherman, like so many Marseillais. The woman had waited at home for her husband to return from the sea. She tried not to look out the windows in the direction of the sea, for fear of seeing an expanse that was absent of him. That was an awful sight, every time. It sent shudders of fear through her. The old man had passed much of his life on the water, on boats, under the flutter and snap of sails. He'd lowered sails and motored into storms and, against all odds, had come out again. He'd been near death at sea many times. And he'd always believed it was the sea that would take him. It would fill his lungs. He would die with his eyes open looking at fish. The sea would give him to the fish. Because for so many years, it had given fish to him. When the time came, it would give him to the fish. This was what the old man believed. Russ knew that this was what the old Marseillais believed. Russ imagined that for years every morning the man had sailed into the port, tied the boat, and at the quayside sold the early morning's catch. The women buying fish had asked,

"How much for this one?" He replied that it was this much. The women said that was too much for this one, for this one here. "It is not a great fish," the women said. And he lifted his shoulders. He said it had to be this much. He said it had been a lot of work to catch this one, this one here.

Russ had moved closer to the couple now, so close that he could hear the breath in their nostrils, so close that he could've touched the old man's shoulder, or his wife's, not her shoulder but her back, gently, higher up on her back between her shoulder blades, and the loose curls of her graying hair. Though he was as close as this now, he did nothing to engage them. Instead he waited for them to begin to move again. He knew that this moment on the quay was over for them and his instinct proved right: in the next moment they turned together and without speaking they walked away from the old port, side by side, somehow knowing where they were going next without even saying the words to each other.

They had not even noticed him. In the way that others on the quay had not noticed him. In a city, people don't see you when you have no connection whatsoever to them. They look right through you. Russ was good at not being seen. He'd been so good at it for so many years that he had few people left in his life. Very few people left. His sister in Spokane was one. But where he lived, in Denver, on a quiet street in the Park Hill neighborhood, none of his neighbors. In his 1931 house, he'd stripped paint from the doorframes and windowframes and sills, and stained these, and refinished the floors. Alone in the house, he did all this work. He'd painted all the walls the purest snow white he could find because he would not stand for a muddy color on the walls, a muddy color would depress him, it would seem too much like decay. Also he'd installed iron security doors, and added bars to the garden-level windows so that the windows could not be kicked in.

His sister did not know he'd been to Ecuador or the other South American countries or all the other places that he'd been for work. For all she knew, he led a simple life working at a home security company, an office in downtown Denver, sometimes installing alarm systems in people's homes. For all she knew, he was dating a woman named Ashley. It was only that he didn't want his sister to worry about him. Now, though, with the cancer in him, there was plenty that she worried about and nothing he could do about it. A doctor, his sister had learned everything about his cancer. He hadn't been able to keep any of it from her. When it came to medical data she was a ruthless investigator. She could be persuasive and tireless. In a series of phone calls she'd uncovered the whole medical story of his cancer, every chapter of it, the arc of it, its heroes and transgressors, and how everyone knew it would end. Everyone knew it would not be a happy ending.

Russ called his sister from the hotel so that she could wish him a happy birthday today on the phone, which was important to her. He dialed into a certain exchange to disguise the call's origin. Partway into the call he said, "It's raining here in Denver," a tricky lie, he knew, because it hardly ever rained in Denver. There was such sunshine in Denver that one could come to believe that there was very little darkness in the whole of the world. He had learned otherwise. "It's crazy," he said, "this rain. Wasn't in the forecast at all. Had to run out and roll down the car window."

"You mean roll it up."

"Right, up, roll up the car windows. A thing like this comes at us over the mountains and no one knows it's coming, and then it hits us. How are things there?"

He wanted to tell her what Ashley had done to him. Would he tell her now? Would he tell her that he'd left Denver, to take this time away? Would he tell her everything now? But it would put a crack in the seal of his lies, it would become a fissure, it would begin to break open all that he'd told her over the years that hadn't been true. He wanted to tell her that Ashley had been unfaithful. It wasn't enough to say that Ashley had lied. It was more than that. When he closed his eyes he saw the photographs again. He opened his eyes. He tried not to blink.

There was soccer. She said, "Well, there's soccer." His older niece was too thin and long-limbed to be any good at it. The younger niece was lower to the ground and fierce. The girls played in different leagues. The leagues were all organized by age. It wasn't a perfect system. Kids of the same age were all different shapes and sizes. Sometimes the kids fell or collided and were hurt, but never seriously. It was harmless for the most part. Russ had shown the older niece how to set up a goal shot, how to be a leader on the field. He'd shown the younger one how to slide tackle the enemy.

That was soccer. Also there had been ballet, gymnastics, swim lessons, and archery. There would be piano lessons. His sister told him she hadn't done any of it when they were growing up, and that's why she was putting the girls in everything. Russ at their age had played soccer. He'd also played the saxophone. Also he'd been bullied. A few times he'd been beat up, but only a few times. He wasn't sure why he'd been bullied except he was always the new guy at school because the family had moved around. He was always being put into new schools. On a schoolyard, when you were the new kid thrown in, you were a target. Most people, both kids and grownups, reacted apprehensively to the unfamiliar. Some reacted disagreeably. A few were bullies, a few in every group. Almost everyone was afraid of change. They didn't want change. They fought it. They preferred the familiar, all that was familiar. Most people.

Maybe this is what charmed him about Marseille. It was full of people who could deal with change. It was something to see, if one could spot that kind of thing. It was inspiring.

7

The Stationer

In Marseille, a widow named Madame de Rouen who endeavored to be kind to others owned a stationery on rue Fontange. The street curved downhill from the Place Jean Jaurès and was lined with such shops. Hers was easily overlooked. It was around the corner from the church Notre-Dame du Mont where, as everyone knew, Chopin had once played. Madame de Rouen did not speak English well but she spoke it well enough to be acquainted with many of the Americans and the occasional Brit. With the Québécoise she spoke French.

Many of her American customers were students. A handful of these were anthropology doctoral candidates, in Marseille for their research phase, about which the Americans could not speak simply enough for her to understand. When asked about their research, in broken French and English they put words together in ways that she couldn't understand, and so it was impossible for her to follow. They were all were like this. Madame de Rouen had come to understand that Americans were not as familiar as Europeans in the way of conversing with those who did not speak their language. And there was no use telling Americans this because Americans were already so impressed with themselves. It seemed that many of her American customers believed their ideas were so big and important as to apply to everyone else in the world. And so Madame de Rouen did not necessarily agree or entirely comprehend but there were many things that she had come to know about the Americans, and all the others.

With an American named Julio she spoke French. He'd stopped in once, but had not yet returned. Sometimes when there were no customers, when she looked out the windows at the people passing on the street, she remembered Julio and hoped to see him. It was a Spanish name, though he was not a Spaniard. He was a journalist from New York City. He did not belong in the same bin as other Americans. When he browsed the pens thoughtfully, astutely, she spoke with him about Haiti, where he'd worked before Marseille. He narrowed down his selections to a Pilot pen and a Ballograf pen, of which he would purchase only one. He sampled each. He wrote actual words, rather than lines or a curlicue as many did. He suggested to her that the Ballograf had a sluggish draw; the pen was *paresseux*. Was it true that the more expensive the pen, the more *paresseux*? It intrigued Madame de Rouen that this question had occurred to him. Though it was not true. The character of a pen was not the same as its class. Other customers had come in. When it came time to make a decision, Julio decided quickly. He chose the Pilot.

Her American customers who were students bought notebooks, loose paper, and pens. The Americans preferred black Pilots. The Brits spent as little money as possible. The Brits bought one pen at a time, never two or three, only one, and a very cheap blue ballpoint that they called clickers. She didn't call them clickers. She called them cheap ballpoints. It was not uncommon for the mechanism to break before the ink ran dry. The French knew better than to buy these. Madame de Rouen cautioned the French. She believed these pens broke as easily as they did because they were manufactured in Chinese factories. Pilots were made in Japan. Once she'd written a letter in French to the Pilot headquarters in Tokyo. She'd written to inform them that their Pilot pens were the most popular among her customers in Marseille, many of whom were from overseas, many of whom were international students engaged in what seemed to be important work relevant to the world at large. She was kind to the Pilot makers. She told them that their pens were better than any of those made in Chinese factories.

To her delight the Pilot makers replied with a thank-you note, hand-written in French, and enclosed a six-pack of gel ink pens, a new Pilot model. Madame de Rouen pinned the note to the wall behind her counter. She reserved the new pens for her own use, though she'd given one of these pens to Ann-Marie Durrante who wrote daily letters to her youngest son in Africa serving in a marine artillery regiment.

The students did not buy pencils. One of the rare customers to prefer pencils was a rumpled old Frenchman, Monsieur Rousse, who sketched scenes on paper while sitting for hours on one of the benches near the Hôtel de Ville or on a nearby low wall with a view of the tourists strolling the old port. He was often mistaken for a portrait artist. He was often mistaken for a gypsy. He did not do portraits. He was short of temper with tourists who asked how much it would cost for him to sketch a portrait. Monsieur Rousse, red-faced, would shout and flap his arms like a startled mouette until the tourists fled. The police ignored him. He was not a troublemaker. He was an artist of street scenes. None of the tourists knew this because he did not have a sign. There was no plaque at his feet that read Artist At Work, Do Not Cross. He made rough sketches. Simple lines. Woman with a little red bag. Man wearing a black hat. A fisherman. A server among café tables. The man who drove the petit train touristique, the train that wound away from the old port and along the sea and all the way up to the Notre Dame de la Garde church on the hill. Often if one spent enough time in the old port, a likeness of oneself could be found in a sketch by Monsieur Rousse.

Monsieur Rousse signed the letter R on every sketch with a flourish, more wide than high, a broad flat letter R, sometimes along the bottom, sometimes along the top. He sketched on whatever paper or cardboard he could find, sometimes a piece of wood. He sketched on whatever material happened to blow by him in the wind that came in off the sea.

One day when Monsieur Rousse was in Madame de Rouen's stationery to purchase pencils, also an American student named Corey was there for Pilots. Corey with some awe recognized Monsieur Rousse and in English told Madame de Rouen that the man was the Bill Traylor of Marseille. She did not know what to say to this. She was not familiar with Bill Traylor. She never imagined that the American students would take an interest in the sketches of old Monsieur Rousse. She encouraged Corey to buy him pencils. Monsieur Rousse could not speak a word of English. But Corey spoke enough French. Corey paid for the pencils, and Monsieur Rousse handed him two sketches in return, simple scenes of tourists in the old port, one of these with a man in the foreground, in which it seemed the man was running through the Place Villeneuve-Bargemon, all signed with the R.

Corey asked Monsieur Rousse in French, "Did this scene occur in the Place Villeneuve-Bargemon while you were painting it?"

Madame de Rouen, regarding the sketch, answered for Monsieur Rousse, saying that such things happen every day. "The man there has left the woman," she said. "See her standing at the top of the steps? There, at the top of the steps by the Pavillon Daviel. She stands there, while he runs away from her. There it is, it is the end of these two. The end of their story. Such things happen."

Corey asked, "Why does he run?"

Monsieur Rousse said, "Sometimes we run because we feel that we must erase who we are. Sometimes it has to be this way." He used the French word *effacer*. He also used the word *gomme*, the erasers in Madame de Rouen's shop. He said, "It is to see if we can find a person worth being other than the person that we have been for all this time. But maybe we find nothing new, only more of the same."

Corey asked, "Couldn't it have a happier ending?"

"It is not a fairy tale," Madame de Rouen said. "It is real life. This is what happens. To want more is not reasonable."

Corey said, "Only, I am suggesting that he runs back into her arms. Maybe this is not the end. He finds a way back to her."

Madame de Rouen asked, "Did he run back to her, Monsieur Rousse?"

"No, he did not return to her."

"You see, Corey?"

Corey said, "Yes, but isn't it possible that later they find each other again? They get a second chance."

"Young man," said Madame de Rouen, "what do you believe will happen? What would you prefer?"

"They will find each other again."

"Perhaps you are right. Perhaps we will see it here from Monsieur Rousse. We will have to wait, because Monsieur Rousse does not draw the future."

Corey and Monsieur Rousse shook hands and left the stationery, both customers sufficiently satisfied.

8

Noémie

Noémie was out walking Chinelo on the leash when, out of nowhere, out of the night and the street's darkest shadows, Noémie smelled the foulness of a drunk and feared that violence was upon her. It was a sense that she had immediately. She inhaled sharply—even before she could look back, the violence was upon her. She was grabbed roughly from behind. A drunk had her in his grip. A glint of street light: a knife? A knife! She tried to pull away! He was taking her toward the shadows. Chinelo yipped under their feet. Noémie struggled to break free but the drunk was too strong. She was being pulled into the shadows. Out of nowhere, such things happened in Marseille.

And the police were usually not around. Noémie had come to understand this. She'd heard stories. And she herself had called to report young men fighting out on the street. She'd called to report family violence in the next apartment. She'd called to ask for help, to intervene, for protection. These were matters of life or death, and the police were not responsive. The police took their time. They were slow to react. Usually they didn't show up. You kept calling, and still the police didn't show up. You called for days and then maybe the police showed up. If they did, it was only so you'd stop calling.

When Noémie explained this to tourists, they agreed. They said, The police moved slowly in the old port. The police did not seem interested in where they were, what they were doing, why they were there.

When Noémie spoke with other residents, it seemed that everyone in Marseille felt this way, that it was not reasonable to expect their police to help them. They had all come to learn this. Whenever Noémie asked, others were eager to talk about it, sharing what they'd heard. Stories of police corruption emerged in the newspapers. There had been scandals in not only the crime-swollen northern quarters but city-wide, at the highest levels.

She did not know the name of this street. She'd walked Chinelo out of her apartment, down and around the winding stairs, and out to one of the many graffiti-covered streets of the Cours Julien. She'd wandered, walking Chinelo. She preferred the small side streets. She felt that she'd walked them all. She did not know all the names. She hadn't been paying much attention to where she was. And now here she was alone on a side street that she did not know well. It was dark at the edges. It was out of the way. It was not a shortcut to another street. It was a side street between side streets. If someone were to pass by, they would not pass through this street but instead would pass by either end of it. They would pass by. There were no late-night bars here, or restaurants or shops. There was no bakery here. Earlier she'd seen others going through the Cours Julien square. But here, no one passed through. She'd left the square, and here all the doors were closed. There was no one.

Noémie opened her mouth to holler for help because there might be someone to help her on another street, but she had had laryngitis for some days. She could not holler. Her scream was a shrill whisper. And there was no one.

She knew that this man intended to take her into the shadows and rape her. Rape was the violence that he intended. He was feeling her body and pulling her. He was stronger than she was, and he was roughly overpowering her. Though he'd been drinking he was not too drunk to do what he wanted to her. She knew that after he was done and after he'd beaten her that he would knife her. He would gore her and then Chinelo. He would leave them both bleeding and dying in the shadows, and then she and Chinelo would be dead, and the drunk would one day do this again to another woman.

And there was no one to help her. But then a bear-like man appeared from out of the night. Bushy hair, a beard. The foul smell of an unclean animal. With a roar this one pushed the attacker apart from her and shouted unintelligibly at him, putting his face close, waving his arms, snapping his teeth. Knocking the knife away. The attacker fled.

Noémie felt a sharp instinct of new fear. She pulled the leash to bring Chinelo closer. What would this one do to her? This insane animal man? This would not be rape. Would he bludgeon her to death? Would he tear away her flesh with his teeth? The snapping of his teeth, the mindless enraged animal of him, sprung terrifying images in her head of what he might do to her. What would he do?

He turned to her. She tightly gripped Chinelo's leash. She could not run, so terrified of all that she could imagine. Her legs would not take her away. How long before he tore the flesh from her bones, how much longer would her limbs be attached? She needed to flee. She needed to break out of this paralysis of terror, but how? She was a little girl again, her father turning to her, her little sister behind her, after her mother had fallen to the floor. There was blood on her mother and blood on the floor. Blood was on her father's hands. Her father, the mindless enraged animal of him, turned to her. What would he do to her? How much of all that she could imagine? There was no question that he would hit her, but how much? And what else?

This man's madness dissolved when he turned to her. A little shyly, he smiled with a strange kindness. In a flash, Noémie recognized him as one of the homeless of the quarter. She'd seen him on the streets. Sometimes on the ground at the wall on her own street. She'd talked to him out on the streets. He was not a drunk. It was only that he was insane. She'd given him her spare change. She gave away things to people on the street. It was her way. After the market, she gave fruit from her bag. Whenever she left a restaurant, she took what was left over and during the walk home she gave it away. She did such things. She had done such things for him.

The bearded man expressed that he was proud to have been able to help her. And Noémie was very glad that over time she'd made the effort to become acquainted with him. It was a reminder to her that it was essential to acquaint herself with the people who existed on her street and the Cours Julien square and the side streets whether neighbors, café owners, street kids, drug dealers, prostitutes, or homeless.

After the incident, whenever Noémie in her comings and goings passed by the bearded man, often in the Cours Julien square, sometimes on a side street, she went out of her way to greet him. He was not clean. He smelled. He was filthy. Bugs were in his beard and on his clothes. He smiled when he saw her. Some of his teeth were broken. But none of this mattered to her. She leaned in and kissed his cheek in greeting.

9

Harvey

Harv Saunders and Bev, while there was still daylight in Marseille, had an early dinner a street in from the south quay of the old port at a restaurant named Le Bistrot Bruit de la Mer. There was authenticity, and then there was authenticity. Authenticity was what they wanted to experience. On this street all the restaurants posted menus in English. At a table, Bev said this was a port city restaurant all right, must be one of these in every French port. This was the everyman of port restaurants. It was very nice, she said, in her way of saying it was an experience she wanted to remember. Harv would remember it but not the menu especially, not the menu as much as the way the reflected daylight shone on the table's gloss and little stars sparkled in his water glass, and the way the waiter's face lit up when Bev asked him what he liked on the menu, what he preferred, because, she said, because she wanted the most authentic thing they had. Harv had no idea what the kitchen was going to prepare for her. She said it had to be authentic, that's all. It could be anything and if she liked it well enough she'd eat it right up. She told the waiter it's why they were renting a room from a family. Anybody could stay in a hotel. But they were renting a room from a man named Pierre and his wife and their children. A family as authentic as could be. Harv suggested that this was the way to authentic, the way was through the people. Harv asked, "You said your name was Nathan?" He stood up and shook Nathan's hand. "Good to meet you, Nathan," he said, and he introduced Bev and then sat down again.

Nathan the waiter said he was not familiar with Pierre's family but he was familiar with houses in the area. On the menu of houses, those in the family's quarter were more comfortable. He recommended them. They had chosen well. Nathan moved the fourth chair to another table but left the third for himself. He occasionally sat with them and when he did they told Nathan what it had been like to stay with Pierre's family. They told Nathan lots of things. They told him that Pierre wore a striped billed hat and had a passion for boats even though he'd never been on one because he couldn't stand on anything that rocked. There had to be flat ground beneath him. He couldn't stand on anything that had a pitch. Pierre had put his arms out and wobbled himself like a surfer. He couldn't do *that*, he'd said. Even the floor of the flat had to be flat, which was why he didn't use the word apartment but preferred the British word *flat*. He'd told them something like this; this was what Harv had understood him to say. Pierre's English was as poor as their French. They hobbled simple words together to convey a meaning. Rarely was there a complete sentence. Pierre had told them he could barely go up in a lift, and they would nod and say *ascenseur*, as if to tell him that they understood exactly what he was saying. Always they said the word *ascenseur*. It was one of their favorite words though Pierre had only ever used the word *lift*.

Always such discussions happened in the kitchen. There were two bedrooms, a toilette, a washroom, a kitchen and the L-shaped hall that connected these. The hall was too narrow for a conversation. They had to file into the kitchen. In the kitchen, a wooden table with two chairs on each side was so close to the wall that Harv could not get himself into a chair on the wall side, but Bev could manage it. At the table, everyone drank coffee from bowls.

There were glass panels on every inner door, with fabric tacked up across the glass. Always in France, Pierre had said, toilette and washroom were separate rooms. After using the toilette one had to go down the hall to wash one's hands, which of course one must do. There was a shower stall in the washroom, a very thin space, just enough room to stand upright, where the curtain hung on a curved pole. Harv could not maneuver in the small space of the shower without his elbows and arms thrashing in the curtain folds.

Pierre said Marseillais were more of Marseille than France. The port is a city of boats, Pierre said. A boat is a city and a port is a boat with a city on it, like wearing a hat. Harv asked Pierre if he was speaking of Marseille or every French port. Pierre said that in Marseille, every quarter is different. There had always been tension with the French government. In the seventeenth century Louis XIV put cannons in the two forts at the mouth of the old port, and pointed these cannons not out at the sea but inward at the Marseillais. In World War II when Germany occupied, the French government asked the Germans to level the poorer parts of the city, and this is why there were now more modern buildings on the north, the Quai du Port side. Pierre said he felt that tension was not the right word but he did not know enough words.

Pierre said even in the middle of Marseille one feels that one is at the beginning, or starting over, like the baby of a chicken with dirt under him. Harv had no idea what Pierre was trying to say. When he explained what he'd understood Pierre to have said, Pierre replied that indeed this was what he'd meant to say. Still Harv didn't understand, but it didn't matter. Often words and phrases were mixed up. Often conversations ended like this one, starting over and again onto something else.

In the family's apartment in the hall there was a picture of the New York City harbor that looked like a photograph but upon closer inspection seemed to have been painted, at least some of it, especially the cruise ship in the foreground with its two red smoke stacks topped with white and blue, and its white decks, more vivid in the sunlight than anything else in the picture. Dreariest of all was the New York City skyline, the buildings softened in the distance under a haze of what seemed filthy pollution more than fog. It was so old that the Twin Towers hadn't yet been put up. And wasn't the Empire State Building standing not quite in the place it should be? And was that or wasn't that the Chrysler building that seemed, in this picture, standing beside the Empire State Building? Something written along the bottom of the picture in script, hardly legible in the dim light of the hall: *Paperliner United States, Flagship of the United States Lines and World's Fastest Liner.*

A jazz band played at night out on the streets of the quarter somewhere nearby the family's apartment, near enough so that it seemed that the band was blowing and beating and singing right under the apartment windows, playing late into the night for tips: tuba, trumpet, drum, saxophone. Sometimes one or two other instruments. Always the same set of songs. Pierre knew the songs. There were only four songs. He sang the words and hummed the melodies to Harv and Bev. Pierre said these men were Roma gypsies and the noise was unfortunate but nothing could be done about it. He said it was like a color of lipstick that Marseille chose to wear. From the windows at night, all night, one heard talking, shouting, and singing. Pierre said people celebrate not tomorrow but yesterday because the day is too hard to celebrate.

Pierre had put in double windows and slept with ear plugs and with a white noise machine running, which he called the "water machine" in English and also the "sea machine" because it made the sound of waves, gentle and lulling. Pierre said only sometimes did he sleep like a boat. Other times he was awake all night. Bev said it was true, that the way a boat floats, it was like it was sleeping, and she'd never thought of it that way and now she always would.

Now in Le Bistrot Bruit de la Mer, Nathan the waiter sat with them, and Bev asked, "What's it like to live here compared to the rest of France?"

Nathan said every piece you cut off the plate has different spice. Nathan said it this way. Marseille is not classic French cooking. Spices come together from all places. Harv pressed him for more. Harv wanted to hear about corruption and crime. Segregation and racial tensions. He remembered that in the film *The French Connection*, Marseille was a hotbed of gangland bosses. It was only a film, and way out of date. But wasn't there some truth to it? This was what Harv wanted to know. At Pierre's he'd asked how often there was gunfire. Pierre had said never, never *bang bang*! Even so, Harv had read that gangs carried Kalashnikovs in the northern quarters. Shootings happened in broad daylight. Armed robberies. Police corruption. Organized crime. Poverty and troubled youth and drugs. Harv could tell that Nathan did not want to speak of those things.

Bev changed the subject: "Nathan, do you have someone?" Harv knew this was coming, because it wasn't in her nature to let them talk for long about the bad that people were capable of. She'd rather not know. She'd rather mark those areas off the map, knowing good and well that there were things she wasn't going to see and feeling that she was better off for it. Harv was different. He at least wanted to know about it. He didn't pretend that it didn't exist. Nathan told her that he lived with a woman. They had two children. He said their names and ages. He said it was important that she and the children had what they needed.

Bev asked, "Not married?"

Nathan said, "We are not of a church."

"Is this typical?"

"There are Catholics and there are Muslims. This is Marseille. And there are others. Marseille has everything on the menu. You are married. And children?"

"We have a daughter, and she has one. That's our grandbaby. We sure do miss them, don't we, Harv?"

"We sure do miss them. We miss being home with them. We call every day."

Nathan asked, "How long married?"

Harv said it had been thirty-odd years.

"You are married for long time." He seemed especially moved. "It is *bon chance*."

"Yes, it is good luck."

"What is the secret ingredient? It is my sister I want to tell." His voice broke, and then he said, "Excuse me, I will for a moment, will return." Nathan left them, and they watched him go into the kitchen and back out again, and then step outside. They could see him light a cigarette.

Bev asked, "Is he all right?"

"I'll just go talk to him." Harv left the table and joined him. He'd sensed that Nathan wanted to say more and maybe it would be easier to say it to one person instead of two. Outside it was warm and the sun was lower in the sky. People were out walking from every direction, from the quay and up and down this street, and out toward the quay, most with purpose on their way to somewhere. Very few strolled. Nathan offered him a cigarette. Harv took it and smoked, though he hadn't in over thirty years. Harv said, "Your sister. Want to talk about her?"

Nathan was staring at the street in the direction of the belly of the port. "Her men have not been good ones," he said. "The pairings are not well made. Like fish, not the same. One fish prepared this way, one fish prepared that way. These fish do not belong on the same plate. She is on the wrong plate. She is at the wrong table. I do not mind to tell you, she works in a bar."

Harv asked, "A restaurant, like this one?"

"No, not a restaurant. A bar, a nightclub. She will know this way only. If she has children, they will be the same. Our children will not go to see pieces of the world. The world is in slices, arrives on warm plates. So many flavors, we do not know what we like, what we do not like. Too many flavors, not everything complements. We do not leave the table. We cannot, because we cannot pay. We are at the table and this is our life. There is nothing else for us. You understand? Beverly asks me what is life here. This is life. In Marseille. For my sister. For me."

Harv said, "Maybe your sister will meet someone. It happens all the time. A man will come into the place and they'll see each other. They'll have feelings for each other. Something like this might happen. Maybe she'll serve a drink to a man who sits alone, and when she does this he'll say something kind to her. Out of the blue, a thing like this will happen, with a simple beginning."

Nathan said, "You don't understand. She does not serve drinks. In Marseille, everything is on the menu. She entertains. This is what I am saying. But she is not lost. She becomes someone else when she in the bar. Even her name is different. She wears names. Like a boat it can be painted on, painted off. It is the same boat, different names. At night she paints on a name. It is what she must do. She forgets who she is, who she was, who our parents are. But she does not forget. I am her brother. I call on the phone. She calls me. We talk and she asks me to call her Sophie."

"You call her Sophie. Is this her real name?"

Nathan shook his head. He smoked, staring out at the street.

"Let me see if I understand. Sophie has a brother. When she uses other names, she pretends to be someone else. It's a mask. A disguise."

"Yes, Sophie has a brother. She is my sister. This I understand."

"Sophie has loved ones," said Harv, and he observed the streets where Nathan stared. Though the light was failing him he felt that he too could see what Nathan seemed to see there: a vapor, a smoke, blowing up, blowing away, blowing around into the shape of a woman who was Sophie, another shape of a woman, and others, all of these Sophie, shapes through which people walked without knowing.

Nathan said, "Tourist men have money. A man buys her drinks and she entertains and on the menu everything is very high price. In the morning when there are no more men and there is no more work then the owner pays her. She is paid her part of all the bills."

"How can she be happy with this life?"

"It is not about happy. Happy is not here. But, to have, the *bon chance* of someone with. Someone with, at a table in the sun. You understand?"

"I do understand," said Harv. "My granddaughter, she's eleven. All I want is for her to be happy, wherever she ends up in life and whoever with. I'd put myself into any trouble if it meant getting her out of a bad spot. Same for everybody I love and I've got to tell you I love a lot of people. Have you considered helping your sister out with a fresh start? Getting her out, starting over?"

Nathan threw his cigarette into the street. "They will find her. Where do I take her, to what city? We cannot go far. This is all we know. You ask what it is to be in a place like this. I cannot leave because she cannot leave and so we are here at this table. I am here for as long as she is here."

"You do a lot for her. You are here for her. You watch over her."

"I do nothing."

"She knows you are here."

"I do not do enough." Nathan crossed his arms. "I never talk so much. Tonight is different."

"How is tonight different?"

"She is in water where there are rocks in the water and waves are coming. Every night is like this. Waves are coming. Maybe tonight maybe tomorrow night, when the waves come it will be too late. And I am a small boat. She knows I am in boat, but what can I do? I cannot stop waves."

When Harv returned to the table, Bev said she'd eaten all the bread and didn't know why she'd been so hungry. "What'd he say?" She wanted to know. "Did you get him to talk?"

Harv didn't want to reveal what Nathan had said because what he'd said had been dark and there was plenty enough dark as it was in the world, for her, for Bev preferred those areas marked off the map, and neither would he want to say those things to his daughter or granddaughter or to anyone else. Harv said, "He spoke of how to prepare fish on plates and how they should be served, and of boats and the sea."

They arrived back at Pierre's before the sun set. The family was not home. Bev and Harv made tea and sat in the kitchen. Bev asked him if he was tired, because he'd had a big plate of food, and because of the time difference, and Harv said he was feeling the time difference a little less every day. He said the further they went, the less important things like how tired he was seemed to be. Harv asked her, "Oughtn't we go home?"

"We oughtn't," she said, "until you see the sights."

Bev stood up to get a closer look at a painting. In the flat there were nautical paintings. Above the kitchen table, on a frothy blue wall, Pierre's wife had put up a painting, signed *F. Porte*, of boats in a harbor. Old buildings on the quay. Harv called it the north side of the harbor because it seemed to have old stone buildings along a *Quai du Nord* that were probably hotels, cafes with terraces, cafe tables under great blue umbrellas, postcard shops, ice cream shops. Harv had become familiar with the word for ice cream shop: *un glacier*. He pronounced it like the glacier word he knew. In this painting, Harv was sure that this harbor didn't really exist. It was a place of the painter's imagination. It could be anywhere. It could be Italy. It could be Croatia. It was just some old buildings behind moored sailboats. And then Harv said of course it existed, it was Venice, wasn't it?

Bev said Pierre's wife had told her that it was Marseille. There was Fort Saint-Jean. She pointed to the low round stone structure at the end of the harbor, with a wall that led off the edge of the scene. So it was Marseille.

Harv said but really it could be anywhere over here. He said it again and then said that was what he had been trying to say.

Bev walked her fingers along the wall of Fort Saint-Jean. She said all the people were missing. The paint was thicker there, she said. So there had been tourists, but they'd been painted out.

High up in the kitchen was a portrait of a salty old captain, white-bearded with a blue billed cap embroidered with a gold anchor. Bev said that this was how Pierre imagined himself, wasn't it? Or how Pierre imagined he would be when older, wrinkled from a life under the sun, having sailed the seven seas, with white hair puffing out from under a sea captain's hat, and that gaze, that look of a man who is looking out at the water and can see the wind and what's ahead and somehow, all at once, everything that has come before. Though of course Pierre was nothing like this. He hadn't had a life in the sun. Pierre's gaze out over the water would be one of boyish longing for what he did not know.

There was another painting of sailboats moored in a harbor, with *NICE* lettered on each starboard, with cypress and rock face among a jumble of red-roof structures, some of these like houses, some of these like grand hotels leading out to the water with open archways and palms, a very clear and colorful scene, signed *J. Ravet*. Bev said, "It's Nice, isn't it? The port name is on the boats." And Harv said, "This could be anywhere over here. It could be just down the coast from here." It was the everyman of French ports.

Russ

In the mornings, Russ took coffee on the hotel's café terrace with a view of the café waiters at odds with the gypsies, the fishermen at odds with the tourists, the police at odds with the thugs. A prostitute wheeled a small bag to a café table and took a coffee to grapple the daylight. All of these usual things. If her night's business had been bad, or if it had been good, she took a second black coffee and stared into the distance where life might be different. For Russ, there was coffee in the mornings, tea in the afternoons. Some days, later in the day, Russ had ice cream at a table in the sun. Not usually the same table. Not always the same café. Sometimes he chose instead to sit out in the open on a bench, with no coffee or tea or ice cream. Sometimes he sat on a low wall or on steps that led up from one street to another. He tried to not have a routine. He knew that no one was watching him. It was unreasonable to believe that someone would monitor his movements in Marseille, but if someone was, then the thing to do would be to not have a routine. Ashley in Alabama had believed that no one was watching her. She was wrong. Being wrong had changed everything. You never want someone knowing where you will be in a moment of vulnerability. You never want someone knowing where you might be, where the best places are to look for you, where you like to go, where you enjoy being. You never want someone knowing your wants.

On this morning at the tables there were five other hotel guests. None of whom Russ had seen before. It was usual to see new faces. Four older French boys on bicycles wheeled past the terrace, while a tourist boy of seven at a table with his parents watched them. It was evident that the boy wanted to be with them on his own bicycle. Always people wanted to be where they were not and who they were not. Almost always these wants were out of reach. When this boy was older, it would be the same. There would always be wants that were out of reach. The four boys wheeled past again. The boys seemed to be up to some mischief but more likely were not, all in the way Russ when he was their age on his bicycle had explored the foothills and the suburban edges, back when everything was different, when land and life had been open to him. That was long before he'd been trained to do all that he'd done. Now, he knew better. That was all. He knew better than to think that land and life were open to him. Things and people get taken out of your life as easily and suddenly as a chimney swift on the wing picks a moth from the gathering night.

A man was alone at a table. A woman was alone at another table, further out on the terrace. A woman might be a man. A man might be a woman. Things were not always as they appeared to be. It was only that it was impossible to trust things to be what they appeared to be. The woman had a purse on the table. Closer in, the man had a camera on the table. The man might be a watcher. Russ was aware that the man had watched him take his seat and this was especially important to note, though it seemed harmless. It really seemed nothing more than one tourist looking at another, as they do, because they are looking for something of themselves. They do this no matter where they are in the world. When they are away from home, they regard those who remind them of home.

And then the man said hello to him. The man was American. Two empty tables between them, five empty chairs. It was a short distance that he, or the man, could cross in less than two seconds. On the table the man also had a newspaper held down by the camera. He could not know if saying hello in return would trigger something unexpected. Sometimes you just have to take a risk and then play out what comes your way. So Russ said hello.

And then they talked about the weather.

After the man joined him, carrying over the camera and the newspaper and taking the opposite chair, Russ learned from their conversation that he and his wife had been in Marseille for four or five days. They'd rented a room in a family's home but then had moved into this hotel. They would soon be on their way in the direction of Spain. That had been their plan at least. Now they were considering their next move. They were on a tour of Europe. They'd started in Amsterdam. They'd stayed in Paris. They were tourists, genuinely, out to see the world. His name was Harv.

Harv asked, "Traveling on your own?"

"For now," Russ said, too quickly. It had been easy to say, though it was imprecise. It suggested that one day he would be traveling with someone, but he could not know if he would ever meet someone, in the span of is remaining life, after Ashley. The man's accent was obvious: the South. So was Ashley. Ashley was of the South, susceptible to its charms. Russ asked, "Where are you from in the South?"

"People can just tell, can't they? People just know it. I don't know what it is. It's like my wife Beverly and I carry around a big blinking neon sign. Alabama, the sign says, look here, Alabama."

It startled Russ: He was seeing the photo of Ashley in a field. There was the photo of Ashley on top of another man. This was Alabama to him. Alabama had taken someone from him.

Harv said, "Guntersville's where we are now. You know it?"

Guntersville was not familiar. Ashley had not been there. But he could not say for sure everywhere she had been. "No," Russ said, standing from his chair. Everything had changed. He did not trust coincidence. This place was no longer safe. Had he been wrong to trust it to be a safe place?

"You all right?"

Russ said, "I'm not sure."

"You need to leave? Bev'll be out in a minute and we're going to have breakfast, if you'd like to join us."

Russ checked the perimeter. There was no indication that others were watching. No one was watching from the boats or the quay or the hotel entrance, or from the quayside streets that led north away from the port. There was only Harv. And Harv had not been in any of the photos. He sat down again.

"I've been plenty of places," Harv was saying. "I was in the Navy."

"You're a military man?"

"Thirty years ago. I've been a married man since then."

"It is not easy to be both."

Harv said, "I never was both at the same time, but I'm guessing that's as true as true gets."

It did not go on for much longer than this. Russ broke away and went up to his room. From the window in his room he could not see the tables in front of the hotel, so he went up to the roof and from there, over the edge, he watched Alabama read the paper and drink the coffee and occasionally say hello to others as they arrived at nearby tables. He watched a woman, presumably his wife, join him. Russ watched Alabama stand from his chair and kiss his wife when she joined him. He watched Alabama and his wife have breakfast and unfold a map and plan their day.

≈

The next morning, when Russ went out to the tables, friendly Alabama was not there. The man's name had been Harv. Russ took the same table as the day before. It was the best table on the terrace, from a tactical perspective. But really he could take any table as long as there was a view of things and room enough to maneuver. Sometimes it was better to be out in the open. When you were out in the open, dangerous things were less likely to come at you from around a corner. Really it didn't make a whole lot of difference where he sat. If people wanted something done badly enough then they found a way to do it. Anything might happen. A hotel window above the terrace might open with a rifle behind it. It was his instinct, it was his profession, to anticipate, but he could not anticipate everything. Ashley had made this crystal clear. It wasn't long before Harv came out of the hotel. It was suspicious timing though Russ tried to put this out of his head. It was only Harv. It wouldn't hurt a thing to be friendly. Russ knew it wouldn't hurt a thing. He in fact needed it. To be friendly was healing. He knew he needed it. Russ waved him over and shook Harv's hand and over coffee they talked first about the weather and then about sightseeing in Marseille. Not long into the conversation, it was clear that Harv was anxious about something.

"Something's bothering you," Russ said.

"My granddaughter got into something. We heard about it yesterday when we called home. It's been on our minds."

"What happened? Is she all right?"

"Ants," said Harv. "She was lying on the grass and there was an anthill. Somewhere out past the back patio. They have a small yard and she likes to be on the grass because it's soft. She walks on it barefoot. She lies on it like it's the softest carpet she's ever been on. She enjoys her comforts."

"I have Kentucky Bluegrass at the house. The sprinkler system takes care of it."

They talked about grass types and full sun, and then Harv asked, "You got anthills?" Russ said that he did not, that ants had not been his problem back in Colorado.

Harv said, "Sitting here I can see Alex lying on the grass as clearly as if I was sitting on the patio right now. Maybe she was counting clouds. I have no idea. She does like to look at clouds. I can't explain why she lies on the grass. Sure, it's soft. It's just something she does. When I was young, I wanted lake water. She wants to be on grass the way I wanted to be in lakes."

Russ said, "I wanted ditches. Trenches."

"That's not one bit unusual for boys."

"So tell me what happened."

"Alex says the ants were all over her arm before she realized it. She started screaming. She tried to sweep them all off. She went running in circles. My daughter grabbed her and sprayed the rest of them off with the garden hose. We knew there were ants. We talked about it. I noticed anthills in the yard the first time I took out the trash, taking a concrete path that shoots straight through to the back gate. A while ago I brought over some ant powder and I told her just sprinkle it on the hills and they'll go away. And of course we have all told Alex to watch out for the ants."

"Will she play on the grass again?"

"Oh, it probably will happen again. There's nothing any of us can do about someone we love repeating a mistake."

Russ said, "She'll be all right, I think."

"We get a second chance at everything, including our mistakes."

"We don't always get a second chance."

"It has me thinking about choices we make, choices people make. Bev and I, we were having supper. We met a man, Nathan, who works at a restaurant on the other side of the port. He told me about his sister. She works in some kind of nightclub. It sounds like she's in a bad spot. Seems to be one of those places where men go to be entertained. Every night, she's lying across an anthill."

"She's not your granddaughter."

"You're right, it's not the same thing at all. But, answer me this, is it choices or something else, is it something we've got no control over, that leads us to the places we don't expect to be?"

Russ said, "If you ask me, it's a bit of both."

11

Noémie

Noémie while passing through the Cours Julien square in the direction of rue des Trois Mages was close enough to the dustup to see that it was two young men. It was not uncommon to see a fight break out in Marseille, even here out in the open of the Cours Julien, in the middle of the day. Because everyone was on edge. The younger ones like these two were on edge as much as everyone else and the younger ones were quicker to fight. Noémie, passing through, would not have stopped. There was no reason for her to get involved. There were plenty of others around. She would not have stopped, but she did when she saw a little dog mixed up in the fray.

When she'd left the apartment her hot dog Chinelo was asleep on the sofa. He'd nosed himself under blankets on the sofa like he always did. When he slept this way, only his nose could be seen in the pile.

The two young men shouted furiously at each other. They threw fists.

Plenty of others were out on the square under the searing sun. Some were men smoking cigarettes at a low wall. At the café tables on the square, eating or taking coffee, under the café umbrellas. Walking with strollers, with children, with dogs. There were plenty of people who might intervene. But as the fight erupted no one stepped in. When a fight broke out, it was like a wind gust, impossible to anticipate, a scene of violence unfolding so rapidly that Noémie did not have the opportunity to think about what to do. She acted on instinct.

Noémie feared that their fighting would hurt the dog yipping at their feet. Noémie rushed in, shouting at them, and snatched up the dog. She took it away from danger. She held it in her arms. It did not struggle. Making a sad whine, it seemed afraid, wanting to be held. She did not know if it was hurt. She'd rushed into fights before. Her nostrils flared. She knew violence. In Montréal, violence had lived in their house. Violence slept in their beds with them and woke with them, and stood staring out the window with them. Violence was in the kitchen. It was in the TV room. It was in the bedrooms. Violence lived in every room. Her mother fell to the ground with blood on her face, and her father kept hitting her. He might kill her. Noémie rushed in and let him strike her instead because she could take it. She could take one or two blows from her father. She did not fight him. She knew better. And then she fell on top of her mother and when her mother woke her there was much to do after this violence had blown like a gale through their home, there were wounds to dress, chairs to stand, broken things to sweep up, a floor to mop.

The two young men pummeled each other, bleeding. Blood dripped from their mouths. No one intervened. One was bigger, and now had the other on the ground, sitting on top of him, punching him in the face. With one of these furious blows, he might kill the other one. Anything could happen. One of the blows could snap his neck, put him in a wheelchair for the rest of his life. Four burly men, nearby on a low wall, could stop the worst of what might happen. Instead these four men hurrahed. They laughed. They hollered out pointers, where to hit and how to throw it. Their amusement and their cheers appalled Noémie though she knew this was the way of men in Marseille. Not only in her quarter. It was this way everywhere in Marseille. This might have happened at Place Castellane with the shadow of the fountain's high monument pointing across the pavement, or along the shops of rue St Ferréol, even where St Ferréol meets Estelle and the big woman in a red dress sings old French ballads for coins, or in the petite cafe square of Place Lulli where it seems a respite from the Opera house district encounters with prostitutes, or even closer to the old port, in the sun-baked plaza of the Cours Honoré-d'Estienne-d'Orves, or on the opposite side of the port with the tourists in the ancient shadows of the Hôtel de Ville. It was the way of all Marseille men and, she knew, as she'd learned, it was the way of most men everywhere.

Noémie shouted at these four, "What are you doing? You must stop them. They are hurting each other. Are you drunks, or are you men? Are you not men enough? Are you not strong enough to stop them?"

With these words, she had struck at their machismo. They grunted and stood up, pumping their arms. They pulled the two young men apart. She knew it was not for her. It was only to show that they could do it.

She asked them, "Who owns this dog? Why did the owner not get the dog?" She was furious that the owner had not rushed in for the dog as she had.

And then they told her what had happened. The one who had been on the ground had thrown the other's little dog against the wall. She said she did not understand, they would need to explain, she wanted to understand. "How did this happen?" She still had the dog in her arms.

They told her, He had been walking his dog, and then the other one had come out of nowhere, picked up the dog, and thrown it against the wall. She looked down at the dog, and it seemed all right. It did not seem hurt. They agreed, The dog hadn't been hurt. It had only been thrown against the wall. They said, "What does it matter about the dog? The dog will be fine."

She asked, "Why did the young man throw the dog against the wall?" No one knew why. The young man could not remember why he'd done it. They said, "Probably it was barking."

She would not give the dog back yet. She was furious at its owner, who was bleeding from his mouth and above an eye. The other was in worse condition. The men said, "Now what?" Because she would not give the dog back. She was angry. She was ready to come to blows with someone. Her instinct was to protect the dog. They said to her, "What are you asking?" But she didn't know what she wanted them to do, only she was feeling the anger and no one cared enough about what had happened to the dog.

Impatiently they asked, "Now you want us to protect the dog? What are you doing? You want us to beat up this one to teach him this lesson?" They pushed the young man roughly. They were on all sides, hemming him in.

It struck her that she would be responsible for this, if she let them do this, the worst of what could happen to the young man. She cared nothing for the young man, the men felt the same way, and truly there was violence everywhere in the world, one could not escape the violence, but she did not want to be the one to cause it here, not now, not this violence to this young man. Instead she handed the little dog to its owner, and then it was like nothing had happened, there had not been a dustup, none of them had ever encountered each other. Like a wind gust stops blowing, everyone went on their way through the Cours Julien square.

12

The Two Men of Rue Saint-Ferréol

On the rue Saint-Ferréol, Marseille's wide pedestrian shopping street, one occasionally sees two men watching the crowd from a wall or from the shade of a recess. These two men are pickpockets, only they don't want to attract too much attention because the police may begin to care, and so the two men try not to take too much of value from people, though really there is not much risk of the police paying such things any attention. Passports were valuable but when lost came to the attention of authorities. It seemed to the two men after some years of doing this work that cash, jewelry, and sunglasses when lost were hardly ever reported. Backpacks were an obvious target. At times working together they were able to swiftly pick a billfold from a backpack, remove its currency, and then return it to the backpack. The currency was not always euros. Often there were American dollars, especially on rue Saint-Ferréol where there was a concentration of international retailers that Americans recognized like H&M, Sephora, and Swarovski. Purses, too, were sometimes much like backpacks, especially when slung over the shoulder and left unclasped. One could reach in.

The key to their work was distraction. Already the tourists were distracted by the shops of rue Saint-Ferréol. Tourists as they walked along were always looking up at the signs. At the port, tourists thronged the quays, but the tourists at the port were not always looking up in the way that they were on rue Saint-Ferréol.

Often the two men stole from each other, and when one caught the other in the act a cheer rose up between them in the Italian way of "Bravo!" It was the same spirit of camaraderie as when watching a football match together, rooting for the same team. Then in quiet French so no one would hear they discussed what had happened, what had been the mistake, so that they might come to understand precisely where the attempt had gone wrong, because if such a mistake happened during their work on rue Saint-Ferréol it might mean a tourist chasing them through the streets.

The American tourists were more likely to give chase. The Americans were less likely to detect the pickpocket's work, but more likely to try to chase him down. The British and Germans were more likely to detect, but less likely to give chase. The Italians were dangerous in any case: quick to detect and quick to give chase. For this reason, and because Italians did not usually carry much cash, the two men avoided Italians. Spaniards never had much cash at all, and though there were many Spaniards in Marseille, there were few who shopped on rue Saint-Ferréol.

One of the two men was older than the other by three years, but this didn't matter in the work. The younger had longer fingers, as if built for this work, but he was a slightly shorter man and so the other had longer arms, a further reach. They were both from Algiers. They could both dislocate their right hand thumb in order to give the hand a different shape. When they weren't working, they regularly exercised their wrist flexibility by pulling their hands back at the wrists for several counts: they counted waahed, athnaan, thalaatha, aarba'ah, and so on. The flexibility of putting their arms behind their back was less important. In this way, too, the speed with which they were able to run was not as important as knowing how to disappear, which was not only about knowing where to hide but also how to hide in plain view and what doors led through to other streets. They wore running shoes. They cared for their feet. Each morning, they rotated their ankles, marched with high knees, warming up like football players.

The two men did not want to ruin anyone's life. They did not intend harm. People were coming to rue Saint-Ferréol for an experience of losing money one way or another. At best, this would not leave a lasting mark, nothing more than an unpleasant memory. The person would return home and be able to say, This is what happened to me once in a foreign city. The person would be able to say, Oh it was only some money.

It was important to the two men to see the effect of their work, when possible. Sometimes it wasn't possible. The person left the rue Saint-Ferréol without realizing what had happened. But sometimes a person did discover what had happened while still there on rue Saint-Ferréol. There was anger. There was shouting, fists up, grabbing people around them on the chance that the pickpocket could be caught. It was a relief to see this. It was a relief to see this person ready to fight. What the two men did not like to see was terror, when the person clutched their bags close, put their backs to a wall. They did not intend to make people feel afraid. The two men did not want people to leave Marseille with fear in their hearts.

The worst to see was despair, when a person crumpled, visibly, at the loss of what had been taken. When there was such despair, the two men discussed in quiet French and agreed to return what had been taken. They did this when the opportunity presented itself, which sometimes was some hours later somewhere else in Marseille. They did this unobserved.

Some of the French on rue Saint-Ferréol were Marseillais, for this shopping street was originally designed to serve not tourists but rather the city's wealthiest residents. In Marseille, this great port and gateway to and from North Africa, because there has always been deep corruption, there has always been a segment of those who have a great deal of money and want to protect their money and their position. These wealthy Marseillais, then, easy to spot, were irresistible. But much care was taken with these Marseillais, because if one of the two men was caught by these and ended up in police custody, no doubt these Marseillais could influence a harsh sentencing in the courts.

Both men were undocumented. If one of them was caught doing their work on rue Saint-Ferréol, probably he'd receive the double sentence, or *la double peine*, of prison time commensurate with the crime followed by deportation to Algeria. Once in Algeria, it then took at least a few weeks if not months to get back into Marseille, back to lucrative rue Saint-Ferréol. A number of plans were discussed on cell phone calls between the one now in Algiers and the one who was still at work in Marseille. They did not expect any one to listen to their calls, though still they took precautions such as, in Marseille, using anonymous cell phones bought in the northern quarters. Money might be transferred back and forth from one man to the other, from Marseille to Algiers or the other way around. The man in Marseille made the necessary bribes on his end that could not be done from Algiers. On the Algiers side, the bribes were less complicated. It was not feasible to return to Marseille by Air France plane, or by ferry. The return to Marseille was by freight vessel across the Mediterranean Sea, always as worker rather than passenger, leaving behind *Alger la Blanche* as the men called it—for it is a white city from the sea, and this sight for an Algerian who is on his way to somewhere else is a profound vision that stays with him always. He ever longs to return to that home.

13

Corey

Corey spotted Evie in the crowded flower market of his hilltop square, the Place Jean Jaurès. The market was winding down, so the time was now not long after noon. It must've been close to one o'clock. Right now back home in New Jersey his father would be on his way home from his day at the office, having left midtown, maybe still on the train from Penn Station or already getting off the train at the station, maybe getting into the car to drive to the house where his mother had set the table for dinner—and what were Evie's parents doing? In what country, in what house? Still he did not know what country she was from. Did her parents worry about her? Did they call, did they want to video chat, did they try to see behind her the room and whether she was still alone after all this time?

Here was Evie in his hilltop square. It was as if the page of a calendar had opened to her. Corey did not follow the days of the week. He did not need to know what day it was. But he knew that today was Wednesday because here was the flower market in his hilltop square. When there was the market of cheap shoes and soaps, of tee shirts and cell phone cases and everything one can imagine that is small and cheap, then it was either Tuesday, Thursday or Saturday. Corey did not follow the holidays, but was made aware of them when he found the café on the square shuttered and had nowhere to take his morning coffee and croissant. Here was Evie. What page of the calendar was this? Evie was going through his hilltop square on her way to somewhere. She was not shopping for flowers. She was not stopping. She was like him. She was away from home and trying to find her way. He could not let her dissolve into a crowd again. He did not want to lose sight of her.

"Evie," he called, but she didn't stop so he caught up to her and touched her shoulder with his fingertips and thumb, pressing gently. She was lean. There was a lot of bone in her. She stopped for him, but it was evident in her look of surprise and the pursed lips that she didn't recognize him. He said, "Evie, we met at the party."

She was not like a flower, not like the market flowers around them that stood in buckets and jars and tin pails, flowers for sale by the stem or bunch. She was not like these. She was not of the countryside, not of fields or mountainsides or shrubland, though in this moment he might be standing with her somewhere on the trail to the Kaaterskill Falls, up in the eastern Catskills, it felt this way to him, standing on the packed dirt of that trail with flowers along the trailside, that time not long before he left for France, alone with Chuck on that trail up to the falls, while he stood as close as he could manage to Chuck and tried to explain who he was. But no one could understand how lost he was feeling, how urgently, and at the same time drawn to so many different kinds of people. No one could understand. Not Chuck. Not even his mother who could otherwise give the name of each of these flowers here in the Place Jean Jaurès. There was her coneflower. There were the neighbor's asters.

Corey did not care for flowers. He knew what a dreary gray this square could be. The flowers dressed up the square only for this morning. After noon the market stalls would come down one by one and be hauled away and then the Place Jean Jaurès would be gray again. There were leafy trees but their color and life were above him; the people here were of the ground, of packed dirt, of pavement. Living so close to the ground, one knew the street, the walls, the ways from one place to another, the tracks of others, the garbage, the smells, the failing light and after all the dark. The people here did not know the summit views. Except the sailors did. Sailors knew these. Among these port people it was the sailors who knew these.

Evie did not seem to remember him. He told her they'd shared moments at the party. There had been a baseball bat. Of all things, a baseball bat here in Marseille. And the violence of the two Senegalese men. He told her how she'd left the room, and he'd stayed behind with the handsome man who was bleeding, and then later he'd found her again in another room.

Corey walked with her. He sat on a bench with her. She was restless. They walked. There was no place he had to be. Not until dinner with Noémie, at their usual place on rue Vian, which was a short walk to the Cours Julien quarter from his apartment. He asked Evie if she would like to join them for dinner. Evie's face lit up and she said she'd love to.

He learned what he could of Evie. She was from South Africa. Her parents were alive and well in Cape Town. He knew nothing about South Africa. She was there in Marseille for no reason. She was not a student. She did not work. She said she was between jobs. He did not learn anything about the work she'd done for money or intended to do.

She was leading him all over Marseille. She had a youthful boyish energy. He couldn't match it. He wanted to rest with her. Maybe even lie down together. She seemed aimless, so at certain corners he began to steer their direction toward his place, and she didn't seem to mind. He did this by touching her arm and touching her back, carefully, as if she might have an electric current.

In his apartment, Corey poured wine for both of them, reaching across the table in his front room where the windows were open and the sun could no longer be seen from most streets in Marseille's La Plaine quarter, except from his hilltop square and a few other high open spots such as the rue des Trois Mages, for the streets of his quarter went up and down around the square. It was clear to him that the Cours Julien square was hers, if any square was. He was closer to the arterial Canebière, closer to the church Église des Réformés and the Jeanne d'Arc. Really she seemed to him off the map. She was adrift on a sea. The wine calmed his nerves. It wasn't long before they were wine drunk, and he felt that he should not have had so much wine. She was no different when drunk. Then they smoked weed while looking down at his street, in the way of his French neighbors, leaning out over the window's balustrade. She was different when high but only in subtle ways. She was calmer, less fidgety. Her eyes blinked more slowly. While they talked, she did not seem to notice that he stood close to her and felt soft parts of her body.

She was looking out the window. He said that the window was worth observing, too. He told her that it happens that each one of us sees something different on the other side of a window, different than what is really there. On the other side of this window, the streets of his La Plaine quarter were the streets and people were people but the two were of themselves and of each other, living off of one another, like bugs in the fur of a beast. Evie didn't say he was wrong. She was ticklish at her ribs. It was easy to make her laugh and this pleased him very much. He told her that he believed that much of who and what each one of us becomes as a person, as a man or a woman, or both of these at once, or even neither of these but as one without gender, very possibly quite alone as a result, well, where was I? Corey said such things. He said that much of who and what each one of us becomes as a person has to do with the place from where we each come. If one is built from the ground up, one must consider the ground. Evie didn't say he was wrong. But it was too simple. He had trouble thinking a thing all the way through and putting a thesis into words. But it didn't matter. She wasn't thinking it through either. She was letting herself be led to these ideas.

So far they had not touched each other, together, with desire, not in the way he wanted to. The more wine he drank, the more he desired her, and in fact the sensations were not dissimilar, the wine high and the desire. He didn't understand what about her was so desirable and somehow this added to her allure. Mystery or something like it was in the air and he was after it. But then it was time to meet Noémie on rue Vian. As they went down the stairs and left the building, an inexplicable shudder went through him. A gritty reality settled. Corey went with hands in his pockets though it was not cold out. He did not trust himself after so much wine and as high as he was to keep from reaching out to hold her hand, to touch her, as they left the building and began down the street to the corner. No one was passing by just now, and the stores were shuttered. Behind them up the street figures could be seen in doorways, a few of them together, a few alone; these were prostitutes. They were transvestites. One of these was Samira. They worked the streets of his quarter, rue Curiol and rue Sénec de Meilhan, and rue Saint-Savournin. Over time he'd become familiar with each of them. There was a blonde. There was the one who wore purple heels. They all smoked cigarettes and there was one who was smoking every time he saw her. He'd say hello when he passed them on the street. He'd stop and talk to them. He asked questions. One said she was from Lyon. The others said they were from Paris but he did not believe them, in the same way that he did not believe they were using their birth names. Mostly Corey told them about himself. Sometimes he paid them to listen to him tell them about himself. Only a few were as interested in listening to him as Samira had been.

Now he was telling Evie about his friend Chuck. He told her that New Jersey people were from all walks of life. New Jersey was like nowhere else, and so a person like him from New Jersey felt like he was of a place that had an out of place identity. A person from where he'd come from could even feel uncertain about what he wanted, what he desired, yes, desire, and where his desires would lead him—a person was not lost, exactly, but aware of the ambiguity.

Evie asked if she seemed to him American.

Corey said she was as cool as a cucumber, and couldn't be more American than that. It made her laugh. He began to explain what these words about a cucumber meant, but she said she'd heard it before. She said it was true, a cucumber is cooler on the inside. She asked, So you say Americans are this way, cold inside? No, no, he replied, only Americans in the movies are cool as cucumbers. She said he didn't seem to know his people very well. He said he was in complete agreement. And then as they reached the corner, to cross in the direction of the Place Jean Jaurès, he was telling her about a time when a street kid approached him with a dead rat asking to use his oven, to cook it and eat it, because there was no other food. Cory gave the boy a euro and told him to get rid of the dead rat. That was all. But at other times he saw this boy approach others in the quarter in the same pitiful way, with a dead rat. People always gave the boy money, and so he kept doing it. Corey said it was true, he was failing to understand people, he was failing to understand people everywhere.

He asked her if she'd seen the boy do this. He was surprised to learn that she had. She suggested that everybody had seen the boy. And she said carelessly, "We all need money. Don't you?"

How had she known? He did need money. He'd found translation work but it was a struggle because he'd learned French conversationally first.

As they walked down the street to the corner, there were no cars. Corey heard a motor, faintly, but it didn't register for him. He was saying important things. The longer he lived in Marseille, the less important the dissertation. He'd never felt so far from the nadir of his ideas. He was ill-equipped to climb to a summit. The dissertation felt like the work of someone else. When they crossed the street, the sound emerged, suddenly loud, as a motor scooter came swiftly around the corner, almost hit Corey, and then glanced off of Evie, knocking her to the ground.

The rider stopped the scooter, but then seemed about to ride away. This way of riding away, of not giving a thought to how it might be for others, was what Corey had come to expect in Marseille. It was the attitude that one has not done any wrong. Things that happen are not a consequence of one's actions. It is not one's responsibility. Everything bad that happens is the responsibility of someone else.

"What are you doing?" he said angrily in French to the rider. "You cannot leave. You must stay, you must stay to make sure that she's all right. You are responsible for what has happened."

Evie was getting to her feet. She said she was all right. She hadn't been hurt.

Corey told the man, "You must apologize to her. You must apologize for what you've done."

The man dismounted the scooter. He was bigger than Corey. He pulled off the helmet. He had an ugly face, twisted in anger. He roughly pushed Corey. Corey fell back against a parked car.

Corey realized the mistake he'd made. He should've let this monster ride away.

Evie shouted at the man, "What are you doing?"

He shoved her out of the way and, with his fists out, moved toward Corey.

But then all the prostitutes came running down the street. They ran fast. They came running and shouting with the high heels in their hands. The man jumped on his scooter and sped away.

They shouted after him. The prostitutes shouted words in languages Corey couldn't understand. And then the man was gone, and the shouting was over.

The prostitutes said they had to speak at least enough in every language. There were certain words, they said, that were essential in their work, and those were words Corey did not need to know, so they would not teach him. Samira was among them. So was the blonde. One of them he had not seen before. Corey did not know how familiar to be with them. He was worried what Evie might think. They spoke with Evie at length, admiring her scarf and her bag and the way she wore her hair. So easily, it seemed to Corey, they touched her arm, her hair.

Evie said Corey had been as cool as a cucumber, hadn't he? She said a cucumber is cooler on the inside. They had to think about this. They said it was an interesting question.

They said they smelled the weed on her. They passed around a pack of Lucky Strikes, which the prostitutes called Luckies. Some of the cigarettes were broken because the pack had been in someone's back pocket during a job. After some time the prostitutes said they could not stay, they had jobs to do, so they went back up the street.

Corey and Evie continued on their own way in the direction of the square Place Jean Jaurès. They went around the corner. And there the scooter man jumped Corey—he'd been waiting for them. He punched Corey in the face, a right-handed jab with weight behind it. Corey fell like a broomstick. The man shoved Evie away and kicked at Corey on the ground. Evie shouted for help.

Again all the prostitutes came running, waving their high heels and shouting that they were going to rip his balls off and put their feet up his ass. But before they could catch him, the man jumped on his scooter and sped away. They shouted after him, and then the man was gone and the shouting was over.

Corey tried to sit up but was in too much pain. The prostitutes knelt down to him and were with him on the ground, and Evie too. They were all around him. They wiped the blood from his face and looked under his shirt and probed the pain in his ribs. And all the while they were still calling that man terrible names, cursing the man softly; it was a chant, and seemed in that moment an occult ceremony among *des bohémiens*. Samira said it was bad. The blonde said she'd seen it before. The new one said that he'd been hurt bad but would be all right.

They all stayed on the ground together and passed around the Luckies. There was no place more important to be.

But Noémie would be waiting at the restaurant, maybe just arriving, pulling out a chair at their usual table and sitting down, looking around. Ahead of him, she would order a glass of wine. She would wait. He could not call her. He'd given his phone to the Senegalese. Corey finished the cigarette and lit another, though he was not a smoker, only it seemed that one should smoke while lying on the ground among this company, in as much pain as he was.

He asked if any of them knew Noémie. He described her as a friend who visits him sometimes. A colleague of his, they were both academics. She was a few years older. He emphasized that she had more life experience. He'd had some life experience but it was true that he was the youngest doctoral candidate in his program. She was a Québécoise who walks her dog Chinelo. The prostitutes conferred with each other and agreed that Noémie was the English teacher who walks a hot dog on their streets and through the square. Corey explained that she wasn't exactly an English teacher but it was close enough. No one knew her well enough to have her phone number. He didn't want to leave them but he felt that he must because Noémie would be waiting.

When he arrived with Evie at the restaurant, Evie would not go in. She shied away from the door like a cat. He took her arm but it was a mistake because she pulled free and he felt as if he'd made a violent move toward her. Though he'd only wanted to touch her, to hold a part of her so that she would not dissolve away.

He said, "I'm not going to hurt you. I could never hurt you. That's not what I want. I'm not capable of it." There was blood on his hand. He found that his nose was bleeding again.

She said, "What do you want?" It was a plea, as if he had a knife to her.

"Noémie's waiting for us. There's nothing to be afraid of. If you don't like this place we'll go somewhere else. I'll go inside for Noémie and the three of us will go wherever you'd like. We don't have to eat. We don't have to do anything you don't want to."

She was shaking her head. She made herself smaller and backed away from him. And then she was gone.

At the table with Noémie the napkins were red cloth. She said, "You're drunk."

He held one of the napkins to his nose. "How do you know that? My head is bleeding," he said.

"It's only a nosebleed."

"Maybe she didn't like the blood."

"Who is this she? Start at the beginning."

After he explained everything, Noémie said to him, "I'm older than you."

"Six years," he said.

"Yes, I know more about life and everything you're dealing with. Listen, she's feral. She bites. It's her way. She'll bite you a lot. It's not easy to hold her. She might never get used to you. You can have her if you want. Sex, I mean. Is that what you want? You can have sex with her. But it will be the end of it because she associates sex with those other men. Men and violence, these go together. And drugs. For her it will always be this way."

"What is sex to her?"

"Violence. If that's what you want, you can do it, but you will lose her."

They drank wine and then ordered something to share, because sharing was what they did to save money at restaurants. Though tonight he was starving and wanted more. This hunger was unfamiliar to him. It was as if there were caverns inside of him, and echoes, slits in rock face that were, in fact, passages from one cavern to another, and unexpected precipitous drops in the dark. It was unusual for him to be so hungry, and he could not stop thinking of Evie. He could not stop thinking of the foreign exchange student during his sophomore year of high school. He'd touched Evie and she'd pulled free of him. He'd wanted to touch her. He'd wanted her to stay with him. He told Noémie these things, and the way the window of his bedroom back home in New Jersey slid up so that he could crawl out behind the shrubbery at the back edge of the front lawn, and in the middle of the night he ran naked through golf course fields. He'd had so much wine that the wine had become like the truth serum of comic books, villains seemed to always have the right tools, like truth serum, the villains were always putting such things together to their advantage, so he did not know what he was saying, as if there were not the harsh realities of their lives kicking at them from all sides like an angry mob.

Noémie was shaking her head: "Wait, slow down, who is the foreign exchange student?"

"Jean. That was Jean." He wanted to keep saying the name. He was pretty sure he hadn't told Noémie about Jean. He wasn't sure that he should. He drank more wine and wiped his mouth with his hand.

"Was this a he or a she?"

"A little bit of both. Anatomically, Jean was a he."

"Are you all right? Is it too warm in here? Would you like some water?"

"We're almost out of wine."

"Are you sure you need more? You were drinking with Evie. It was to get drunk. Was it because of her?"

"She's not to blame. Jean was from Marseille. You've seen me drunk a number of times." He counted on his fingers. "At least three times."

She asked in French if they should speak in French or English. Which did he prefer?

"It's not fair," he said. "You are better with the language. You have more words. I don't know all the words for feelings."

"You know the words," Noémie said. "It is not the words. What did Jean tell you of his home in Marseille?"

"Jean talked a lot about the boats and the sea. He described the place where his family lived. He said there were other families. So his family did not live in a house. He told me this much at least. His family lived in an apartment. He could walk to the sea. The sea was like a member of the family. The sea was a sister he never had. He spent time with the sea, sitting beside it, talking to it, listening to it. He watched it come and go. He told it secrets."

"What did he tell the sea?"

"I wasn't there when he talked to the sea. That was before I knew him."

"All right. Go on. What else?"

Corey said, "At our house he liked to walk from room to room. He would leave his room and go into the kitchen, because that's where his room was, off the kitchen, like a servant's room, I've always thought. And then Jean would go from the kitchen into the dining room and into the living room and through the halls and into other rooms, the library, the office, the pantries. In the walk-in closets he would turn on all the lights and look around at all the clothes and all the shoes and everything, my mother's scarves, so many of them, all colors. And he would go outside, to the patio, to the lawn and across the lawn like some divine creature walking water, it's the way he walked, and through the kitchen garden, through the flower garden, so many flowers, he would smell them all, all the way to the gazebo. And of course there was the back gate to the woods and the paths that led away from the house through the woods until there were other houses, other people, others who had their own foreign exchange students."

"And you," Noémie said, "let me guess, you followed him around the house. Wherever he went?"

"Of course I did. I couldn't help it. He was a strange magical creature that someone had let loose in our home."

"What was his magic?"

"Everyone liked him. He was likable but there was something more."

"He was different," Noémie said.

"We get plenty of different in New Jersey."

"But Jean was different in new ways. He was different in ways that you needed at the time."

"Why are we talking about Jean?"

"Because you followed him everywhere. All through the house. Did he know you were following him?"

"Yes."

"Did you follow him into the woods?"

"What are you asking? Yes, woods, there are woods behind our house, there are paths that lead to different places. You go into the woods and you walk around and you end up in unexpected places because woods are like that."

"Did you have a relationship with Jean?"

"Ah, that's what you want to know. What does it matter what we did?"

"Because you followed him to Marseille."

"No, not exactly."

"Something drew you to Marseille."

"Marseille is where everything is converging."

"I can see that," Noémie said.

"The academic work led you and I both here. It is important work."

"Have you tried to find your Jean?"

"I have no way of finding him."

"Wouldn't you like to?"

"Yes, of course, that would be interesting. But I have no way to find him. He liked comic books. I didn't speak French but I read all of his comic books. And he read mine. He spoke English. He could read and write better than he could speak. He sometimes wrote the words to me. It was easier for him sometimes. I still have some of them. Pieces of paper with his words."

"What do they say?"

He pulled out his wallet and found a small fold of paper. "This one says it is dangerous identity to be who I am where I am from." He returned it to his wallet. "It makes no sense but at the time it made all the sense in the word."

"The word you like is identity," she said. "Or maybe it's the word dangerous. Where do you think Jean is now? Still in Marseille?"

"He could be a grill cook at a diner in middle America. He could be anywhere."

"But you think he's here. Do you feel that he's here?"

"He could be anywhere. It's not unlikely that he's here, in Marseille, somewhere on the streets. Yes, if I think about it, I would say he's somewhere out on the streets of Marseille. He's not living on the streets. He has a home. Of this I am sure. He has a home and he spends his time on the streets. He's out there being a part of everything."

"You have stopped bleeding but you have blood on you." She wet a napkin in her water glass and wiped his face with it. "I did not know all this about you."

14

Harvey

Three stops into Europe and the only thing left for Harv to do was lose their passports. He saw no other way home.

"You have to see this church," Bev said to him, her finger tapping a picture in the guidebook: it was the Notre-Dame de la Garde. It was the church up on a hill that everybody could see from everywhere in Marseille. Harv could see it well enough from where the two of them were sitting on a café terrace in the old port. They'd go up and tour that church, but it wouldn't mean much to him. After all this sightseeing, Harv was starting to get what his brother, who hated churches, had meant when he'd said the next time he's going to church is in a coffin.

"You have to see this," Bev said to him. It was only that Bev wanted him to see all that he could, while he could. Already he had no night vision. There might not be as much time left as they'd hoped.

From Amsterdam they'd tumbled down through Paris and landed in Marseille like something heavy fallen out of a tree that broke itself on the way down. At least that's the way Harv felt about it. Bev's take was different. This was her chance, too. Harv just couldn't put it on himself to deny her these experiences abroad. He'd never seen her so happy.

In Holland they'd taken a bus out to stand looking at a whole field of tulips. They did have some of those in their yard back home that bloom dutifully every year. She really wanted him to see the whole field of them. And then Bev just about knocked down every passing Dutchman asking where they could find a windmill to look at. They never found one. "Pancakes," she'd said to the waiter at a canal-side café, "I'll have a tall stack of them and see how they're different cause you know Harv here uses real butter." And then to Harv: "This will be something to see." At another Dutch café she'd asked of their apple pie, narrowing her eyes, "Now you don't put nothing funny in, do you?" She expressed with utter delight that she didn't like any of it.

In Paris at one of those St-Germain cafés she'd said to the monsieur, "Now just bring me a strong black cup of coffee the likes I can get over in Louisiana where there's more French than you can shake a switch at." The monsieur had suggested that stick was the common expression rather than switch. She replied, "Now, let me tell you, a switch is a stick but it's the one your daddy makes you choose for your whipping. It gets picked right off the tree cause a dead one'll break across you."

"A special stick," said the monsieur.

"I tell you what, it sure is special."

"And what does this have to do with the French?"

"Oh, lots. There are lots and lots of you in Louisiana." When he left, she slapped Harv's knee. She sure was happy.

Harv said, "We could've just gone over to Louisiana like you said. Brought Alex with us."

"You don't fool me for a second," she snickered and opened the Paris guidebook.

Right then and there at Marseille's Place Lulli where they stopped to rest, at ten minutes to two, then and there his name was Harvey Saunders, and hers was Beverly Luella Saunders. Tomorrow they would have no evidence of this. It would be hell, but then all better.

When Harv drops their passports in the sea at the mouth of the port, when he does this without Bev seeing it, up around Fort Saint-Jean's walkway, he will be cutting out from under Bev the trust that she has had in him during the whole of their thirty-odd years of marriage. Or he may lose the passports some other way. He may lose the passports to the sea over the side of a ferry while on their way out to whatever Marseille has in the way of a field of tulips. He may lose their passports to the sea any number of ways. But lose them, he will.

Harv checked the daypack. He'd brought them here by way of rue Saint-Ferréol, the busy shopping street. He'd left the pack's outer pocket unzipped. An easy job for a pickpocket. But it was not as he hoped. The passports were still there.

Bev rested back in her chair saying, "Heavenly," with a sigh, positively beaming. "I just don't know how it would be if you didn't get to see all this."

Harv suggested, "Maybe just push me around in a wheelchair."

"We could do that and I bet we'd get treated better."

"Don't you want to go home?"

"Home's always there, Harv. Home's always there. Home's always there. When we get back, we'll wish we'd seen more."

"Our pancakes," Harv said. "Our coffee. A pad of butter. Maple syrup from Vermont."

"Say it with me, Harv. Say home is always there."

"It is, that's true, no doubt about it. But we could cut things short—"

"You think I'd let you take me home? A woman's place is by her man in trying times like this. Anyway, you know as well as I do that our syrup's from Winn Dixie."

"What if something goes wrong? Promise me if something goes wrong we'll just get on back home."

Harv was trembling. Bev checked his head for fever. Harv said he was all right. But he'd never been so nervous. Not even the day he'd gone into the Navy and taken the bus to Huntsville to do it, or the day he'd gotten out of the Navy and faced a whole lot of nothing ahead of him. Not even the day he'd asked Bev to marry him or the day they'd done it.

It was now about the time that they made the phone call to Alabama, so Bev called on their cell phone and talked before it was Harv's turn to say hello. "Here he is," Bev said into the phone, leaning toward him with it, "I love you, here he is," and Harv accepted the phone laughing, cajoling Alex even when she asked him why her grandpa had to be so far away, when she said it wasn't fair, even when she said they were missing her eleventh year, until Harv couldn't anymore, Harv couldn't speak. "Tell your grandma," he managed to say and handed the phone back to Bev who had teared up and was chewing her lip, as she did on these calls. Harv imagined she was chanting in her head, in the face of such sacrifices, *Home's always there,* in the way that she was able to, so much better than he. It was different for him: home was far away, and time was running out.

Bev had their daughter back on the phone and told her it only takes a lump of butter in the water and some salt and pepper, and then you just leave it alone for a while, uncovered, enough flame to keep it going. They went on like this about cooking, though their daughter knew how it was all done, only it softened the edges of the pain of being apart to talk through it. And then Bev told her they'd be leaving Marseille day after tomorrow to continue on through Europe.

Bev didn't know yet that they would not be taking the train first to Montpelier and then on to Barcelona, as they'd planned, not if Harv could stop them.

After the call Harv and Bev over coffee and a wedge of chocolate cake talked about their daughter and granddaughter and things that were happening back home. The wedge was an elaborate cake. It was spiced. There was nothing plain about it. Harv couldn't place the spices. Bev found it delightful. Harv would've preferred it plain.

It occured to Harv that it was time to arrange yardwork at the house. They decided to send a message from the hotel to Trevor, the neighbor's son. Trevor already knew they'd be asking for his help and in fact he might've already done the mowing of the front and back, and the trim work around the two trees and Bev's flowerbeds. Trevor was a sophomore and the best guard their Guntersville Wildcats had under coach Fred Steger. Those games wouldn't start up again until October and they were really something to watch, if one was able.

After Harv lost the passports, he would need to discover that they were gone. Maybe in the middle of the night he will crawl out of bed and make enough noise rifling through the daypack, dumping its contents, so Bev will wake up and ask what's wrong. With his foot he'll sift through the stuff on the floor, and he'll say, "The passports. They're gone." He'll sigh. Or maybe he'll throw himself into a rage, break something, hurl a chair at the wall. But none of that rage business was who he was and might make her suspicious. So he'll just sigh. Whatever he chose to do, she'll feel enough of a jolt.

The day after, they'll go to the U.S. Consulate and report their passports lost, or stolen. He'll be at her side and she will be anxious, impatient, perturbed; the officials will be unflappable. She'll say that back home in Alabama things got done. People were efficient. People knew how to fix things when somebody needed help. Why couldn't the officials fix this right? Did the officials have nothing to say about it?

The officials will say, "We're helping you. We're working on it. Here are the things that must be done. Do these things and then we can help you."

There will be forms to fill out, identification to present. It will be exhausting. Harv will pay all the fees. Bev will be infuriated by all of it. They'll need new passport photos. It will all be too much. It will wear them out, but it will jar her enough, and then she'll keep her promise. They'll go home. He'll see more of the morning light on the front lawn, when he goes out to the porch for the newspaper, the dew glistening on the grass. That was what he'd like to see, more of that. When he thought of failing light, he thought of Alex running across the lawn at fireflies, the way she did that, the way she shrieked happily every time one lit up. She'd run toward it with her arms out, even though every time it was the same ending. She would never find it in the air, she would never get her arms around a firefly.

&

Harv had no night vision. He was no longer in the early stages of what was happening to his eyes. So they did not go out at night. There were other reasons they did not go out at night. Harv had read in the guidebook about areas of Marseille that were unsafe. When it was daytime in those areas, his wallet might go missing. Their cell phone might vanish from his daypack, her wallet from her purse, or anything at all from inside her purse. But after dark, pickpockets weren't the concern. Danger was thrilling when it wasn't as real as this. One might get beaten and robbed. One might get beaten, robbed, and shot.

He and Bev agreed that they were obvious targets. They had American tourist written all over them. It was written all over them that they were not savvy world travelers. But they felt that they knew enough of the world to know what was safe and what was not safe.

They played out what might happen: if and when someone snatched Bev's purse, Harv was to give chase, but not for long. He was not to go far, because he was sick. He was too sick to give chase, Bev said. If he did start running, he shouldn't go far. Certainly he should never leave her sight. It would be best to not give chase. Instead they should call 911. But, did 911 work in Marseille? Would anyone pick up? Harv did not know. Harv found nothing in the guidebook about it. So if something happened they would have to find a policeman and report it. That's what they would do, they decided. Probably she should not carry a purse, and instead they should carry everything they needed in Harv's daypack. It was less likely that someone would try to snatch the daypack from Harv, or the camera. Bev turned over her jewelry to the hotel front desk for safekeeping.

Harv was not willing to put loved ones in danger. He wrote down a list of the dangerous areas: between this and that street, or in the vicinity of such and such landmark. Some of this was guesswork. He marked all of these clearly on the map. It narrowed down their options. There was much less to see of Marseille.

Each day after an early dinner while there was still daylight they did the long walk that Harv had always liked to do after a big meal, a walk in which the route, the sights, and the destination were not as important as the pace, the steepness of roads, and the distance.

On this day after dinner, long before the sun went down, they walked from the old port to the Palais Longchamp, but not by way of La Canebière and Boulevard de la Liberation as one would expect, but instead in a roundabout way beginning in the Belsunce quarter and after seeing the Porte d'Aix triumphal arch at the nadir of the expressway to other places where they would not be going anytime soon, they turned in the direction of the train station, Gare Saint-Charles, and wandered the streets of this quarter, finding themselves up along rue Jean de Bernardy for some blocks and then at rue Louis Grobet crossing to Boulevard Longchamp J. Thierry. This was a long walk though still it was well worth going more distance so they went past the Réformés church up the steep road rue Saint-Savournin to the hilltop square Place Jean Jaurès.

Already they were planning for tomorrow's day to include a visit to the Musée Cantini to see the exhibition of Roberto Matta, the Chilean surrealist painter. Harv did not know what to expect but from reading about it he understood Matta's life work to be politically charged, taking on some really tough subjects, like the French government's savage use of torture during the Algerian War. Harv agreed that art was important and meaningful work and he was proud to feel this way because, he knew, not everyone felt this way.

The museum, Musée Cantini, had been closed for some time for renovations. It's re-opening with this exhibit was one of the many programs part and parcel of Marseille's designation as the European capital of culture for this year, 2013. Back home in Alabama, in Guntersville, Harv and Bev didn't have access to cultural institutions of this scale, though a few times in recent years, since retirement, they'd driven over to Birmingham, which was not real far from Guntersville, and once they'd brought their granddaughter Alex with them, and they'd seen some exhibits that had come through as well as the permanent collections. Bev did not like to spend as much time in the museums as Harv did. Bev said that she preferred to be out in the sun when the sun was out. Harv remembered an exhibit of Danish pottery, of bowls, teapots, and vases. And he remembered an exhibit of southern quilts. They had seen such things. He felt that it was good and right to see something of oneself or the history of one's people whether it was easy to look at or not.

Harv and Bev had been in Marseille for more than seven days and this much time was not what they had planned. By now they should've been in Barcelona already for some days. By now they should've seen the sights that were recommended in the Barcelona guidebooks. By now they should've climbed the Church of the Holy Family, *Sagrada Familia*. As one would expect, by now they should've had brandy in a café and then gone up in those towers together, with too much alcohol in them and the blood boiling, in those narrow and treacherous passages, climbing. But something held them in Marseille. They had moved into a hotel on the port. They chose a hotel on the north side because a view of the port's south side was more picturesque with its old buildings and behind these the rise of the land and in the distance, not real far away, the church up on the hill. Sometimes in the middle of the night Harv stood at the window over the port to see what he could see, while Bev, he knew, pretended to sleep. They did not know how long they would stay in Marseille. On some mornings they talked about it and decided to stay a day or two longer. Something held them. The meat of it went unspoken and neither knew how deeply the other felt about this. But they had a pretty good idea. Having been married for so long, they had a sense of knowing what the other felt without needing to talk through it. Each knew the other was not ready to leave Marseille, whatever the nuanced reasoning. Each knew that something held them.

In the mornings Harv went downstairs some time ahead of Bev while she finished getting ready for the day. He went out to one of the hotel café tables for coffee. At the hotel a newspaper in English was complimentary so he read news of places closer to home, with his coffee, while others did the same, other tourists, some of them speaking English but there were other languages, too, and some of the others were men alone and some of them couples. Many of them had a guidebook or a map on the table. Always Harv said good morning to the server and to any customers who happened to look at him. It was the way he was built. He couldn't keep himself from saying good morning to others, in the same way that he couldn't keep himself from holding a door open for a woman or an elderly man. He liked to think that he was doing the right thing. To say good morning was like holding open a door, inviting someone to talk. The other person might kindly say good morning in return. The other person might say a thing or two more. They might talk about the newspaper headlines. This is how he'd met a Colorado man named Russ on the hotel's café terrace. Russ was traveling alone and didn't have anybody to talk to, so Harv began to join him for coffee when he saw him out there. Russ had two nieces around the same age as Alex, and Harv wished they could all get together and meet one another back in the States.

In the afternoons Harv and Bev made a call on their cell phone to Alabama. Alex asked again when they were coming home, and when she'd ever see them again. Bev said to her, "Soon, Alie, soon."

Alex did not understand where they were, why they weren't with her, why they'd left her. For Alex it must've seemed that they'd left her behind. She was no longer loved. Something about her now was no longer worth loving. This was clear to her because they would not return to her. If she were worth loving, they wouldn't have left her behind. She didn't care about Europe. She didn't understand what about Europe was worth more love than the love they had for her. If Europe were another girl, she would beat up Europe. She really would. But she knew Europe was not a girl. Europe was not something that she could understand. All she could understand was that she was no longer loved.

Their days in Marseille were divided by the time before this call and after this call. Immediately before this call they would have lunch at a café and unfold the map and browse their lists and guides and they would plan for the rest of the day's activities. Always the plan involved walking some distance though their feet hurt now, their legs ached, a dull pain seeped upward into the very core of them.

On this day when they arrived at the hilltop square Place Jean Jaurès, Harv ached all over, the steep rue Saint-Savournin had been hard, he was exhausted, he was out of breath, though none of this was the sickness in his eyes, it was only that he he had too much weight on him from the sedentary life they'd led in Alabama for so long, for their thirty-odd, really for their whole lives. He stumbled, tripping over his own feet. The pack seemed heavier now. His back was wet under it. The camera that he wore with the strap over his shoulder hung awkwardly under his arm at his ribs. The camera strap had rubbed red lines into his shoulder. At the edge of the square he felt so fatigued that he lost footing again, stumbling into a Frenchman. He said he was sorry and tried to explain that he was tired, but his French was no good. The man wasn't angry. The man suggested the pack was too heavy, touching the side of it, and then he continued on his way. Harv pulled off the pack to sit on a bench. He set it on the ground at his feet and the camera, too. He sat with Bev close beside him, under a leafy linden tree, to rest after the distance they had come, with the sun falling lower in the sky and long shadows in the square. It seemed to them that lots of people were going through the square. The hilltop square was, clearly on the map, on the way to so many other places. A Frenchwoman with a kind smile, who had a dachshund on a leash, asked them in English if they were all right. Harv felt warmed by the goodness of this gesture. The dog licked his pack and then she scolded the dog, and she stooped down, holding the dog with one hand and wiping the pack with her other. Harv said, "No worries, no worries at all." And then after they were alone again Bev said that it had been saintly for the woman to ask if they were all right.

From their bench in the hilltop square Place Jean Jaurès it was all downhill and so the walk from there was easier, the work of pushing up steep roads was over, as they made their way back down to the old port and the hotel before nightfall.

In the middle of the night Harv woke with a start and turned on the bedside lamp. He did not know how it had occurred to him, whether he had dreamed his way to the realization or if the good sense had simply come to him. He hastened out from under the covers, off the bed, and over to the chair in the corner where his daypack was.

"What's the matter?" asked Bev, getting up on her elbows.

But Harv was too alarmed to speak just now. He dumped the pack's contents on the floor and sifted through those things with his feet. He dropped the pack and turned away. He picked up his pants that he'd left over the back of the chair. He scrunched the pants in his hands. There was nothing to be found there. He dropped the pants, the belt buckle clanked. He said, "My wallet." Bev gasped fearfully with a hand over her mouth. He kicked through the stuff on the floor again, and then searched through the empty pack, all of its pockets. "And goddammit the passports too." It had happened after all. He threw the empty pack at the wall. He was furious with himself. How could he let this happen, after all? He made fists and might break the chair or tear down the curtains with his teeth or rip something to shreds, but he didn't. The rage just as quickly boiled down.

Bev asked quietly, sitting up all the way, "How is that possible?"

He took two long breaths and it helped. He was thinking it all through. "The wallet had to be since dinner. The passports, I don't know." Harv was now resigned to it. It wasn't his fault. It was only that there was evil in the world. Hands on his hips, he was not as angry now. He simmered. He lifted his shoulders. All he could say was, "It's Marseille."

Bev said, "The man who bumped into you."

"The woman with the dog," Harv said. "Remember her?"

"Oh no, it couldn't have been her. She was nice to us."

"Did she reach in? I wasn't watching her hands." Harv sighed. "I guess we can't know. What time is it? Nearly three. Well, no use trying to sleep. My eyes won't even close now. I'll just see if anybody's down at the front desk. I'll call down first."

"Everything," Bev said. "Lost."

He shook his head. "Not everything."

"Who we are. How do we show who we are?"

She couldn't get all the way dressed. He could see it sinking in to her, the stunting significance of what had happened. It tore him apart to know all this would hurt her as much as it would. She would blame herself, and that would hurt her. And then she would blame him, which would hurt her later in a different way. She would come to blame them both. But then she would blame Marseille. She would blame all the people they didn't know. She would anchor herself with the knowledge that something like this wouldn't happen to them back home in Alabama. She was trying to get dressed. She was going through her things because all of this was sinking in and she couldn't decide what to wear, what occasion this was like—was this like dinner out? A walk on the quay? A boat ride? What to wear? She was confused, trying to figure it out. And terrified. He'd never seen her like this and didn't know what to say to help her. She turned to him with almost no clothes on and asked, "What are we supposed to do?"

"I don't know. They'll tell us." He fastened his belt. He pushed his feet into shoes.

She said behind him, "We can't get on a train or anything. We can't leave, Harv. How are we supposed to get home?"

He tied his shoelaces and began to button his shirt. "We'll find a way home." He was pretty sure that she'd never seen him like this either. He didn't want to go on anymore.

15

Russ

Russ Bower's story with the woman who was called Sophie, though it was not her name, began in Marseille's old port under a hot sun on a café terrace with a view of the mouth of this great marina of sailboats, fishing boats, and ferries. From the belly of the port, ferries took tourists in and out to see the limestone cliffs along the coast, cliffs that cut in and out, shaping the calanques. Those were tranquil bays where one might swim and take pictures of one another with the scrubby maquis up on the rock face, and Aleppo pine trees and olive trees. A respite from the mire of Marseille. The limestone cliffs were white to him. They were variations of white. There was gray stone, there was gold stone. Russ didn't know the language of color, so he didn't have the words to describe what he'd seen, but what he felt was that the rock face was of lighter tones here than others he'd seen, in other far-flung corners of the world. Sophie's hair was not blonde but it was a lighter color than Ashley's, and about the same length. Russ would like to think that there was no more Ashley in his life, in his consciousness, but when he closed his eyes he saw the photographs again. She was always there, like radio waves. He couldn't get rid of the signal. This woman Sophie whose hair was lighter than Ashley's was welcome interference.

Russ and Sophie's story began on a café terrace with small cups of strong black coffee and boules of ice cream. He took the table next to hers. She had already been served. He could see that she was eating the menthe ice cream. When the café owner came around, he ordered the same. He did not know why he took the table next to hers. He did not know why he ordered the same flavor. He found the flavor refreshing. It was just what he needed. A ferry was heading out to sea, this one to the Château d'If and then to Port Frioul on the Ile de Ratonneau. Tourists with their cameras were on the top deck and aft, and looking out from the starboard windows. Russ hadn't been on one of these, though he'd been out to the calanques. He'd hired a private sail. In one of the tranquil bays, he'd asked the French sea captain named Laurent to heave to and let the sailboat drift. There were other tourists in their own boats gaping at the place. Russ could not know if these other tourists felt all that he felt in knowing there would be no chance to experience this again, this was the first and last time, this was a measure of a music that was quieter now and falling away to a subdued finale. While Laurent watched the wind and the water. Could it be like this, at the end? Was it Laurent who would ferry him to the other side? There was a small beach and from the sand some young French in blue jeans and black shirts and sunglasses waved at him and called out to him. In simple English they called out to him for cigarettes because they had run out. He had none to throw over to them. It was not a hardship, not this, for these few young French to have no cigarettes today, but there would be hardship for them, there would be plenty of hardship, one day if not today. Over time water had cut at the land and shaped these limestone cliffs. It was impossible to comprehend for those of us who do not live very long. Our passage of time is microscopic. Hardship would cut at these young French and shape them and one day others will heave to before them to regard the effect of it, but not comprehend it. Such was the way of the world. Russ asked Laurent if there were cigarettes on the boat. There were not. Laurent did not smoke. Russ said, If only there were cigarettes I would throw the pack over to them.

But the calanques were not part of his story with Sophie. His and her story began late in the day on a terrace. These were marble tables and round cane chairs with blue-striped padded seats. He'd never seen her before. He felt that he would've noticed her elsewhere had she been sitting alone like this. He wouldn't mind getting to know her. Probably she could detect this. Probably she had guessed that he was traveling alone. Probably she was guessing that he was feeling lonely and miserable, the way it gets sometimes when traveling alone. One begins to feel that areas of himself are caving in. He began to feel like a hole-ridden block of Swiss cheese. He feared that he could no longer hide it from people. The sun was falling in the direction of the sea. There was a little dog, a long-haired mutt. It wasn't hers. It wasn't interested in her, not like he was. It wasn't interested in anyone. It was going around and under the tables with its nose down. It wore a red kerchief. The café owner carried things on a tray to a family at a nearby table. The owner had long graying hair, old faded jeans, his shirt sleeves rolled up, and a leather strap around one wrist, a boho bracelet. He was at ease with everyone in a way that was infectious; everyone was at ease with him. The family's child asked if the dog was a garçon, and the owner with the round tray against his chest said it was confusing, wasn't it, because of the kerchief, the kerchief made him seem like the waiter, but the dog wasn't the waiter, it was only a dog. And the family laughed. This was how Russ had understood their French. He spoke French well enough but had only half-listened.

Russ, smiling, let his gaze fall away from the owner and the family and the dog, and he happened to meet her gaze at the next table, her gaze falling away from them, too. Her lips: a smile. So they shared their amusement and also the wholesomeness of the moment, everyone at ease with each other, everyone at peace, a moment in which it seemed there was nothing to be very concerned about in the world because at the core of humanity there was goodness, and those things in the world that had gone off track were surely on their way to get back on track. The areas that had caved in could in fact fill again. It was a sensation the likes of which Russ very rarely experienced. And he felt sure that it was not a common sensation in Marseille where there was such agitation among the peoples, at so many cultural intersections, crossings, overpasses, underpasses, where there were collisions, where there was a turbulence that at the very least, at its lowest point, was like the unease, the restless foreboding, that would keep a fisherman from taking out his boat, one could feel this tension among the residents of Marseille very nearly physically as a vibration in the air over the old port and the arterial Canebière and the churches and the mosques and the cafés and all the city's quarters.

There was nothing Russ wouldn't have told Sophie that day under the hot sun—anything she asked, anything at all, the worst of him, the best of him—but she didn't seem curious. She asked nothing to draw out the things that he didn't want to say. He ordered a second boule of the menthe ice cream and ordered one for her, too, though she said she couldn't, it was too much, it would put weight on her. She protested mildly in French, and to this he said that she was a thin woman, with no weight on her to speak of. She said this was not true. She said that one must grow old and fat. She said this in English and it rang true to him. It really was that simple. To this he said that one must breathe. He was embarrassed to say this because it was out of context. It sounded disingenuous. This thing about breathing was an odd thing he'd been occupied with for some time now, something to which he occasionally turned his focus. It helped clear his head. One must breathe. He understood this to mean that there is one's life, and then there is the end of one's life. There will come the end of one's life. Things happen unexpectedly. Like loss of a loved one. So, one must breathe. Here the phrase was an awkward reply to her but she didn't say so, she merely said *Merci*, with a faint blush, as if kindness was something she was not very familiar with, something that she never expected, something that surprised her when it came to her even a small way. But this faint blush elided something rough about her, he suspected, and probably also it was the way that she closed her hand, made a fist, when he then suggested that they share a table.

He said he appreciated the company, that he wouldn't mind talking more in English, that it had been some time since he'd spoken English so easily with someone French and her way of speaking reminded him of his sister in Washington state, while boats came in and out, while the sun baked them.

He did not know what to say to Sophie, to entertain her and put her at ease. It was his training to calculate one's reaction, though not usually like this; his work, in private security, was usually in dangerous places, with dangerous people, to varying degrees. He didn't have a lot of experience in circumstances like this one, in which persuasion was the tactic with the woman at the next table to engage him in conversation. In a way this felt more dangerous. He began simply, the only way he could think to do it, by telling her that he was American, from Colorado. He said that he'd come up out of the ground there on the plains just like the mountains had. This had been his mother's way of saying it. The woman, whose name she had not yet shared, liked this way of saying it. A man could come up out of the land like a mountain. Not all men. She smiled. And then he talked about his family. He told her what his father had done for work, and about his mother, and his sister who was now in family medicine in Washington state.

Sophie had a small tattoo on the inside of her left wrist. It seemed her instinct to keep it hidden from the world: her left hand rested in her lap, and when she reached with her left her palm was down. But he saw the tattoo. He was trained to see such things. It was the letter Z, or N, stylized. Or it was simply a design of two lines, connected. So, possibly there had been someone else in her life, someone who was now gone. Because usually such a mark was about memory and the past rather than the now or the future.

She told him that she was from the Cévennes, from Hérault. He did not know what this was. She explained that the Cévennes are a range of mountains. She was from a village not far from Montpelier. She said her name was Sophie, though it was not really her name. He did not press her on this. She said that she had changed her name for her work. He found that she had a way of looking away when she said things that she did not usually say to someone.

There was something odd about the work that she did. He could tell that she was conflicted: she did not want to talk about it, yet she must, and she must do it sooner than later, because somehow if she didn't and if he didn't understand it right away then it could ruin everything that was beginning between them. And so, conflicted, she did not reveal it to him.

It was the same for him, with the cancer. He did not want to tell her about the late-stage cancer that was spreading fatally from the skin of his left arm through the whole of him even during this brief span of time at the café terrace. But he must tell her sooner than later because if they fell closer together and then when she learned of it later the news would be a blow and the knowing would tear her to pieces and ruin everything that had happened between them. He could not bring himself to speak of it. She could not know that under the sleeve of his white linen shirt there was a scar under which there was a cancer that would take him away before she could love much of him, if it came to love.

❧

Russ Bower and Sophie, who had only just met and did not know each other well, walked together on the quay on the north side of Marseille's old port. This was after talking at one of the many cafés, talking for over an hour, it might have been two hours, sometimes laughing, he'd tried to make her laugh, and while they'd talked at the café he'd felt warmth and had revealed things that he would not normally reveal to a stranger, and he felt that she had done this, too. It was the way it is sometimes for two people who are instantly at ease with one another. A spark of something had happened and was happening between them. It was why they had decided to share a table, to be closer. He'd left his table and, at hers, took the other chair.

Now they walked together past café terraces, hotel fronts, souvenir shops, and the lone tree on this quay. Others were strolling and thugs were watching and youth were speeding past on bicycles but these others barely existed for him while he was with Sophie. He and Sophie were not holding hands or touching, though it felt to Russ that they could, that they would if he reached out for her hand, but he did not. The sun was lower behind him and just as hot on them as where they'd been moments ago at the café. On the quay side of the Place Villeneuve-Bargemon, a rumpled old man on a bench caught a page of something blowing past. The old man was writing or sketching—was he an artist? A portrait artist? Russ felt an impulse to ask him to make a portrait of Sophie. No, it would be a portrait of the two of them together. And in doing this they would stand side by side before the old man. Russ would put his arm around her waist. This is how they would first touch.

But that is not what happened. Russ did not stop them at the artist. He considered all of that as they passed the Place Villeneuve-Bargemon, as they passed opportunities, and then they were passing another café terrace, and then more of these, and hotel fronts, and souvenir shops, and Sophie was asking him to tell her more of what he'd seen of Marseille. He wanted to tell her everything. He told her that yesterday he'd followed two old Marseillais, a man and woman who walked together on the quays of the old port. He'd followed them in the opposite direction than he and Sophie now walked. Sophie seemed curious to know more. She said that she wanted to understand why he'd followed the man and his wife. Had he talked to them? He said that he had not. Why not? Usually there was a good chance that he'd speak to someone but yesterday he'd been in a particular mood because the day had been one of some significance for him. What had interested him about his encounter with the old man was their difference in perspectives, the difference in perspectives of two men who are nothing alike, who come from very different worlds to the same place, who have very different relationships to the place. He believed that the old man was a Marseillaise, and a fisherman all his life. He'd been one of those who sold their catch on the quay. Russ had imagined that the old man regarded the old port, which had always been the center of this old man's home, and the old man regarded its changes, marveling at how a place can change so much over time. And Russ said he'd detected a fear, too, in the man, a subtle fear that the place would continue to change so much that one day he would no longer recognize it.

Sophie said, "You have an imagination."

"It is a preoccupation."

"Did you imagine an ending?"

"No, only my own. I was feeling older yesterday."

"And today?"

"Young again."

"Why do you say he was a fisherman?"

"The way he looked out over the water. He could see the wind. The wind reaches out for the water. The water reaches up for the wind. It's like they hold hands, these two, the wind and the water. It's always been this way through all of time and he could see this."

"I think different," she said. "I think the wind hits it." She opened her hand with the palm up and struck it with her other hand. "Like this. The water, she lies there and takes it. What choice does she have? She cannot go anywhere."

He slowed down. He was disturbed. "That's an unusual interpretation."

"I'm silly," she said, smiling. "I like your imagination. What else do you imagine? What of me? Am I fisherman?"

He could not put anything to words, he hadn't expected the question, and he was concerned about the question that might come next, *what do you imagine of us*, and so he could not find words. "Silly," she said again, she laughed, and then they laughed together and she touched his arm when they were laughing.

They reached the Quai du Port where it ends at a broad pedestrian quayside at the belly of the port, the Quai des Belges and Quai de la Fraternité and the broad pedestrian area between them. This was where in the mornings fishermen sold the morning's catch, as they had for centuries. Russ had browsed on some mornings but he hadn't bought fish. Instead there, each day, Russ bought a lilac branch from a young Roma gypsy girl. As he and Sophie reached the Quai du Port where it ends, he turned with Sophie in the direction of the broad quayside, but Sophie hesitated. She looked that way and then looked away, not exactly in the opposite direction, but away, and from this and from the expression on her face he could tell that she was thinking about something unpleasant. She was uncomfortable. It could have been fear.

The Roma gypsy girl with lilacs was there now. The girl approached him, holding out to him one of the cuttings, while cradling in her other arm a bundle of other cuttings. Probably the girl recognized him. As was his way, he asked her how much she was selling it for, and then he gave her that and more.

He thought to give the lilac to Sophie. He considered how such a gift might be received in the context of what was beginning to happen between them—and then, Why even think about it, did the gesture need to have such meaning, why not just do it, why not be an incautious man? Indeed he felt conflicted at his every action, worrying that he would make a mistake and ruin everything.

And here when he'd stopped to buy the lilac, Sophie had stepped some paces away. Was she bolting? He knew better than to try to give the lilac to her now.

Sophie said she could not go that way, she would not. "It is not good for me," she said. It was mysterious. She did not want to walk on the quay at the belly of the port in the direction of the port's south side. The Opera House was over there. What else? Russ did not know. He felt that he could not ask her why it was not good for her to go that way. It was a moment in which they might part, a terrible moment. He did not want the passage of seconds to unfurl an ending to his and her story.

She chewed her lip nervously. What was her fear? He could only hope that she, too, did not want an ending. She stared at the white church on the other side of Quai des Belges. He asked, "Have you been inside this cathedral?"

"This one? This one is not a cathedral," said Sophie. "I used to go in the churches. I used to think it important but this is no use. I'm not like the others."

"The other what?"

"French women."

"How are you not like them? Because you don't go to church?"

"We can be with many people," she said. "But, stay alone, as many people ourselves."

"I don't understand."

She did not seem able to put it into words, and he did not press her.

He offered, "How about this way?" He pointed the other way, uphill, the rue de la République. She turned with him in that direction, they waited for cars before crossing, and then they continued walking. They were silent until he said—and he didn't know why he was saying it, this seemed aimless talk—that the other day further down this road on the wall of a rehabbed elegant apartment building he'd read "A Squatter" in spray paint, and he'd interpreted it to be a signal from the people that no one would be moving into these buildings, and wasn't it a fact that the very people who were working on the rehab of these buildings were the people who were being economically pushed out of the quarter, and wasn't it just the way the cruel world works, and then he said anyway what he'd wanted to say was that he knew that he'd paid too much for the lilac. The price didn't concern him. He bought one every day from the girl and her mother, and always the mother said thank you to him as he left them. It was only for a table in his hotel room. And every day by the time he stood it in a glass of water it was already drooping and faded, its leaves curled, and of course he'd known that he bought it well on its way to decline. Each morning the hotel woman who cleaned the room discarded it. Each day he bought one to replace it.

As they walked up rue de la République he carried the lilac along his arm. Sophie said, laughing lightly—her laugh was a wonderful music to him—she said that he was carrying it like an infant. She'd said the French word enfant, which could have a broader meaning than the American English infant. The French word could mean an infant or any young children. Infant here as he'd heard it carried more significance. He would not have thought much about the word baby, or the French word bébé. But to him the word infant carried the significance of what was happening between them. He held it aloft and agreed. He said it was pink like an infant.

He had not expected this to happen in Marseille. He was prepared to deal with almost anything else.

They turned on Grand-Rue, going further uphill, and onto rue de la Caisserie, in the direction of the old quarter Le Panier, in the direction of the cathedral, in the direction of the sea, while he told her more about his family, his late parents, and his sister in medicine, his sister's husband, and the two nieces, who were the only few people left in his life. He told her that he'd met a tourist at the hotel who had a granddaughter, and that back home they were going to do their best to arrange for the granddaughter to meet the nieces, even though they were on opposite sides of the country. They would find a way. Sooner than later, if possible, while there was time. Before it was too late. Because the young are only young for so long. He almost spoke of his cancer but he did not. He could not bring himself to speak of it. He could not evade the invisible presence of his cancer. Its presence was disorienting. It was loud in his ears while he talked and walked, and while he listened to her, watched her, looked ahead at the road and the hill, and while he thought about where they were on the map, and to where they were heading.

A surge of panic, like an ocean wave, nearly took him under. He could not walk any further. He stopped, and Sophie stopped beside him, on the rue de la Caisserie before a pink stone building with much decorative stonework, and ironwork at the windows—it was unmistakable, the Pavillon Daviel, for he'd been this way before—a building with a magnificent wrought iron balcony and black doors. Here he told her while he wrung the lilac his hands that he regretted to say it but that he must part because, because he was scheduled to make a phone call at this time. Words were failing him. He told her that he must return to the hotel at once for this, he must return at once, because already he was late for the phone call.

"Ok," she said, leaning toward him, without hesitation, as if the necessity of his departure was a matter of fact, as if he in fact was late for a phone call. He nearly questioned the necessity of it himself, the necessity of a phone call that did not exist, because she did not question it. Though she must have known it was not true for it seemed to him that clearly he'd fabricated this. Clearly he was being evasive. For all his training, somehow this lie did not ring true. He could not make it ring true. And then, without hesitation, she kissed him on each cheek in parting as people do. If she sensed that he had no phone call then she made no indication of it. In her eyes he recognized the sadness of their parting and this was in her smile, really in all of her, it was in the way she stood before him and the curious slight tilt of her head and in the way her lips were apart. "Well," he said, and could not bring himself to say more. He could've said to her how wonderful it had been to meet her, to spend this time with her, this brief time. But wonderful would be too weak a word. There was not a word for it, not in any language. He could've said something so that she might think of him and wander this way again. He could've left some way for them to find each other, some clue for her. He could've mentioned the name of his hotel, but he did not. He could not bring himself to say anything. Fear gripped him. It was a fear that if he said something more, then he would not have the strength to part from her, and then they would fall together, and then she would be hurt—she would be hurt either way but this was less than the greater hurt that comes later with the loss of someone after falling together, after being together for days, months, years, after love has had time to seep down to the bones.

Russ hurried away down the steps of the broad and open Place Villeneuve-Bargemon. In the direction of his hotel, he nearly broke into a run. He looked back. He could not keep himself from looking back at Sophie. She had not moved. She was watching him leave her. And then he saw what may or may not have been a great and unfortunate trick of the light, a glint of light on her cheek—Russ would consider this for the remainder of the days of his life— something on her cheek like a glass bead, in this light, falling.

16

Corey

In the Cours Julien quarter, on rue Crudère, there was a bar with live music. It was just around the corner from Café Vian where Corey had many times met Noémie for wine and his favorite dish the cassoulet, and where he'd last seen Evie. Corey had never been inside this bar, but he often passed by it. At night out on the streets, he'd heard the noise of it. He hadn't been able to see what it was like inside because black plastic was over the front window and the front door's glass. The bar was Pussy Twisters. The front window was pasted with fliers for bands like Hair and the Iotas, Shun and his Dead Family, The Sicilian and Cassidan Disasters, The Dirty Farmers, and Mistaken Sons of Alabama.

Corey needed a drink after the day's tedious work of putting Marseille in the context of the Harvard dissertation. The piles of papers were so dry they crinkled. He felt dry, too. The papers seeped the oil from his fingertips. Evie was like something of his dissertation work. He grappled with what she meant to him, trying to get at an understanding of who she was. He unpacked her phrasing and looked for what was missing. He dissected the meaning and relevance of her. But the context was all wrong. Without proper context, his theoretical work fell apart. He knew nothing about her family or South Africa or what occupied her. Evie was there in Marseille for no reason but to torment him.

But all this was not complicated. He was making it complicated, because he was confused. He did not understand what it was that he was feeling. He wanted to take her apart to understand her but he couldn't figure out if what he really wanted was to disassemble the history of her or take off her clothes, or both, or which of these first and then the other. The sexual impulse was clear. His head confused the signal.

The wine bottles in his kitchen were all empty. Corey piled these up in a cardboard box to carry out later. He searched the rooms of his apartment for more wine but found none. It was getting late. He looked out the window at the streets where she had looked out with him, the night he'd last seen her. It was no use looking for her out the window. He decided to go to Pussy Twisters. They would have wine. He went through his square Place Jean Jaurès—where it had been Wednesday, for in today's flower market for some hours he'd waited on a bench telling himself that he was not watching the crowd for Evie, and he'd bought lots of flowers that he could not name—and then along rue des Trois Mages and rue Trois Rois, to rue Crudère, passing rue Vian. To get to this bar that was, really, off of the square Cours Julien, which was Evie's square, he might've gone another way. By way of rue de la Bibliotheque for example, or even rue St.-Michel and Place Notre-Dame du Mont, if time was not a problem. Because there is no reason to always go the shortest way, when there are so many ways, it is better to walk different streets, to experience the city in different ways, always, to take one's time, this is the way of the Marsellais after all, but, as thirsty as he was, tonight he went the shortest way.

Corey did not know beforehand that, at least on this night, Pussy Twisters was a biker bar, something that was immediately obvious when he stepped inside. Everyone but Corey, even the women, some of whom as burly as the men, wore black leather, black tees, black leather vests, bandanas, dark sunglasses pushed up onto their heads, more leather, the Harley Davidson logo, and tattoos, lots of tattoos of naked women, and tattoos of naked women on bikes. Slogans on jackets like, Ride it like you stole it. If you need me I'll be riding. Hold my beer while I kiss your girlfriend.

These were motorcycle aficionados. They were Marsellais with a particular passion that Corey had never imagined might exist among the French. But here they were. They converged in this neighborhood bar to hear loud rock n roll about the road. They were talking about the bikes, the gear, the rides. Always the rides, the roads of southern France under the sun, in the clear air, with the views, with the wind. Sometimes the mistral. Sometimes the ride was difficult in the mistral.

Just inside, Corey hesitated and almost walked out, though not because these were bikers. What concerned him was the Confederate flag behind the bar. He could either walk out or he could stay long enough to find out why this flag was behind their bar. He decided to ask them about it. He walked up to the bar with his hands in his pockets, and he greeted the men there. The men were gruff. He wanted wine but ordered a beer. It did not seem the place to ask for a wine list.

He asked them, "Why the Confederate flag?"

A barman said it was their symbol. It was the symbol of Pussy Twisters.

Corey asked, "But why this flag?" He explained to them that it was the flag from the American Civil War, a flag of the Confederate States, the ones who had lost the war.

Yes, they said, they knew what it was. They said it represented freedom to be whatever you want.

He was handed a beer. Corey explained that this flag was one of his country's most controversial icons, and had come to represent opposition to civil rights.

They argued that it represented freedom.

Corey explained that he was not from the Deep South, in fact he'd been raised in New Jersey, and understood less than he probably should about the history of the flag and the complexities of its controversies and interpretations. He drank beer, and he explained that it did not represent freedom. Instead it represented a certain identity, and though malcontent the character traits of that identity were not those of the typical Marseillais. The traits of that flag bearer's identity were not desirable, and certainly not of those in present company.

They argued that it was only a symbol of freedom for the people of Pussy Twisters, it was only a symbol of the place, of the radical attitudes of the Cours Julien, and all of Marseille, freedom, a symbol of being whatever you want to be, whether you play in a band or live homeless on the street, or you go into bars and drink beer and argue about their flag.

Corey said that this was an example of two things that did not go together, two people from very different places. These two people did not belong together. It was unfortunate and there may be parts that are attractive, certainly, parts that seem irresistible, but one must consider—they interrupted him, waving their hands. They said he was dismissed. The school bell had rung. Class was over.

Corey with his glass empty ordered another. He asked them if they had seen the Matta exhibit at Musée Cantini. This exhibit marked the reopening of the museum, after more than a year of extensive renovations. They had not.

Roberto Matta, Corey explained, was a Chilean surrealist painter. Matta's later paintings were more political. His *La Question* painting that denounced torture during the Algerian War.

Corey said, On the premiere étage, there is a painting named *Alabama*, in which Matta recognized the civil rights struggle of the states. "My country," Corey said. He told them that they must go to the Musée Cantini and see this painting, and then decide whether to take down the flag.

They said, Why should we take down the flag? It is freedom to us, the freedom to be whatever you want to be. This is what the flag means to us.

Corey told them to go to the Musée Cantini. He asked them if they had seen the work of Monsieur Rousse. They interrupted him, waving their arms. Monsieur Rousse, they repeated, Monsieur Rousse. They pursed their lips, mocking Corey, walking back and forth with hands on their hips repeating the name of Monsieur Rousse. They laughed. They howled the name of Monsieur Rousse.

Corey said that he would bring them art by Monsieur Rousse and they would see. But he would have to get the two sketches back from his friend Noémie. He'd given these to Noémie because he did not hold onto things. He could not find things he wanted to find. He could not hold onto things he loved. This is why he'd given the two sketches to Noémie. Get rid of the flag, he told them. Erase what is there. Replace it with a sketch of the old port by Monsieur Rousse. Find Monsieur Rousse and commission him to put up one of his windows over Marseille. He downed the rest of his beer, and on his way out left euros on the bar.

He felt worse somehow. His thirst wasn't sated at all. He wandered into the square Cours Julien and walked along the low wall where people were sitting. None one of them were Jean. But one of them was Evie. He felt a jolt inside of his chest. He sat down beside her. At first she didn't recognize him. He agreed that it seemed darker tonight than other nights. It was so dark that it was not easy to see who people were, what they were really about. She said that she did recognize him, and that she remembered their long walk together and his apartment. She said it had been sweet. He recounted their times together. He told her they'd almost been killed by a maniac on a motorbike. He said if he'd been killed then his parents would've never known how happy he'd been in that moment. They would've come for his body, and his few possessions, but they would have found that nothing explained his state. It's what they would be most curious about. They would not care about his work, his dissertation, his papers and his books, though they would go through all of these looking for clues. They would not care about Marseille. They would find it very difficult to hunt for clues about their son in this foreign city, which was not as tranquil as he'd described to them during their video chats. But still his parents would try to find clues. They would talk to his neighbors. They would see people on the streets—up the street figures would be seen in doorways, a few of them together, a few alone—and it would be these who knew him better than others, but it would never occur to his parents to ask the prostitutes about their son. His parents would not know where to look for clues, because they had never been able to understand him. If all this ever were to happen, his parents would find no clues.

"My father works in the city," he said to Evie while he took her hand. He squeezed gently the soft parts of her hand, feeling around for the bones. "He takes a train, and there are some nights he works later than other nights. There are nights he comes home very late, because the later it is, the less often the train runs. That is what we have always been told. The train schedule is the reason that he comes home late. Sometimes the company puts him up in a hotel because there are nights he has important work to do very late and then again early in the morning. It's not what you think, or so I thought. When I was old enough it wasn't difficult to find him at the bar in Delmonico's with another woman, and another time with another woman. He does not know that I know. I did not take pictures of them. I did not follow the women or try to find out who they were, or how he'd come to know them, though I could have. I could've learned about them, but they were not as important to me as he was. There were so many questions I had. Why did he think that my mother could not do these things with him? Or did he do things with these women, did he ask them to do things, that he felt were too unclean for my mother? Is he sick in some way? Does he have an addiction that my mother cannot feed? Doesn't he, after all, love my mother and isn't it part of loving someone to let them feed you what you need?"

Evie lit up and passed the joint over to him.

"Thank you," he said, taking a drag and passing it back. He would teach her how to throw a baseball, as he'd taught Jean.

She said, "You can keep talking. It's better than nothing."

"It keeps the night at bay, doesn't it?"

"Yeah. And the noise of cubs."

"Cubs? You mean children?"

"You hear them? Over there somewhere."

Corey listened for it.

17

Harvey

Harv Saunders stepped out of the hotel and, blinking at the brightness of the new day, he stood among the terrace tables. It was a new day but for those who did not enjoy the freedoms that he did it would be the same day again and again. He was ahead of Beverly who needed about twenty or thirty minutes more to get all ready for the ferry to L'Estaque, the daytrip they'd planned. Harv had the camera. Bev would bring down the daypack. He did not want to go to L'Estaque after all, but he would go. He felt that L'Estaque was an odd detour on the way home. The past few days had been rough on Bev, but it was not clear yet that she was ready and willing to feel the same way. They'd been to the consulate, filled out the forms, made the necessary arrangements. They did what they were told to do. In another day or so, they would be given papers in place of their passports. They would then have identification enough to board an airplane. For now they were killing time and it felt to Harv that they were occupying themselves in such a way that it didn't matter much what they did. They'd done enough sightseeing. They had plenty of pictures. It exhilarated him that the time away was running out. He was hopeful that Bev would soon join him in feeling this way, and then they would be making a clear plan to return home. He didn't know what best to do with the time left but there were good things that he was capable of doing, if only the right opportunity would present itself.

Now he was ready for a hot cup of coffee and some breakfast. Bev would come out and eat something, too, before they joined the ferry line on the quay. Something might get in the way of their L'Estaque plan for the day. He wouldn't mind if something did get in the way that would do good for someone. He'd been awake most of the night recalling his Navy days, and thinking of all the things he could've done better in his life and all the things he ought to have done differently. His thoughts kept coming back to all that Nathan had said about his sister Sophie's situation. There was nothing Harv could do to help. He understood this. He could not sail into a port to rescue someone from a bad spot. It was not who he was. It was not who he'd ever been, his whole life. He understood all this and it did not please him. He wasn't a bad person. But he'd had opportunity to be a better person than he'd been—where had that opportunity gone?

At the tables, people were having coffee, bread, poached eggs. People were reading newspapers. People were staring out at the quay and the boats in the old port and, further out, the church on the hill. It didn't seem like such a new day. It was the same as every day. Whatever had happened last night at such places where Nathan's sister worked was finished and done. There was nothing he or anybody else could do to change what had taken place. Harv was hoping Russ would be at one of the tables, and there he was. Russ waved him over. Harv joined him and ordered a coffee from the server. Russ ordered another coffee as well. They exchanged pleasantries. Russ seemed tired, like he hadn't slept well. Harv noticed that Russ had cut himself shaving, and mentioned the cut was still bleeding. Russ said, "I guess I'm a mess this morning," and dabbed the cut with a wet napkin.

They sat in silence looking out at the port. The coffees arrived right away, and Harv said, "I was telling you about Nathan's sister. The one who's in a bad spot."

"I remember."

"I've been thinking about her, and the fear that she wrestles with. Her name is like the name on a boat, painted on. That's how he described it. Every night before work she paints on a name to be someone else, to be different. She walks out the door of her home every night a different person. She feels that she needs to be different."

"Different than who?"

"Different than Nathan's sister. Different than a woman who feels that she's alone, with little to no hope of finding someone to love. But she does have loved ones. She has a brother who loves her."

"If only that was enough to protect her."

"Yes, if only that was enough. But it's not." Harv was turning his cup of coffee on its saucer, and then he said, "I fought a lot when I was young, my Navy years, before our daughter came along. I had to settle myself down. I was a natural. I wasn't some kind of nut. I wasn't out looking for fights. It's just that I was good at taking a punch. I've always had a good constitution. Becoming a father, now that was a different fight. Those punches are harder. Took me years to feel like I was worth anything as a father and in truth I still struggle with that. Life would certainly be a lot easier without loved ones you have to watch over."

"Well, Harv, you say it's easier but for me today is less easy than yesterday."

"What do you mean?"

"Oh, nothing. You were saying."

"Do tell me," said Harv.

Russ hesitated, and then said, "I met a woman yesterday. That's all. It didn't work out."

Harv insisted he say more. He wanted Russ to tell him about it.

Russ said, "She and I had that spark that people speak of. It flared up between us. So strong, that spark. And then I couldn't stop what happened next, we couldn't stop talking, we knew we could be with each other. We both wanted it. It happened so fast. She was wonderful. I don't have the words to describe her, or my feelings. We were perfect for each other. But I had to let her go. I had to walk away. And so I walked away from her. I knew I had to walk away as clearly as I knew that we were perfect for each other. It was one of the hardest things I've ever had to do. That was yesterday. Today there is regret and confusion, but somewhere inside of me is relief, too, for having the strength to do what's best, no matter how painful. What you say about life being easier without loved ones, it's not. It's not any easier. I can tell you that and I can back it up. But sometimes it just has to be that way to protect them. The last thing you want is someone on your side getting hurt."

"People don't mind taking some hard punches for the right reasons."

"What are some of the reasons?"

Harv tapped a knuckle on the table. "To do good for someone."

Russ looked away. It was like shaking his head. "Most people are on their own."

He hadn't told Russ about the retinitis pigmentosa. When his eyes failed him entirely, when the world's light no longer fired signals to his brain, for the rest of his days, how would he be able to do good for anyone? Instead they would all be helping him. He would need a lot of help. Things would have to be prepared for him, brought to him. He would be useless. There would be routines. Around the house the tables and chairs and sofa and side tables would be fixed in place. Bev would take down all the family photos they'd hung over the years. Family photos would be another of many constant reminders that he couldn't appreciate such things. Bev and everyone would be careful not to change a thing in the house. Really nothing would be different one day than it had been the day before. Ahead of him yawned a future of routine. But at least he would never be alone. He said, "I'm losing my sight, Russ. It's the real thing. It's an eye disease and there's no cure. I'll be blind soon. It could be sooner than we think. And that'll be it for me, Russ. I won't be much good after that."

"You're telling me you're sick. I had no idea, Harv. I'm sorry to hear it."

"Well, it is what it is. There's nothing I can do about it."

"It's why you're in Europe, isn't it?"

"That's it, this was all Bev's idea. See the world before I can't see a thing. She's doing this for me. We'd much rather be home." Harv let that sink in, and then he said, "I don't get why you walked away from her. Because one day you'll be glad to have someone with you. You keep taking these punches. I have to tell you that it's not a worthwhile fight. When you meet someone, that's special, isn't it? Why fight it?"

"Maybe you're right," said Russ. "I'll let it happen. I'll turn this around and get together with her, when our paths cross again." There was no light in his eyes when he said this. Harv didn't believe a word of it. He sensed that Russ was holding something back. Russ said, "But that's the thing, you see. There's no way. Our paths won't cross. I don't know anything about her except a name, which is a common name. I could ask around. I could try to find her. And I will, I'll try to find her, I'll sit in the café where we met and I'll walk where we walked, and I'll do everything I can think of to find her, but I already know I'll never find her again. This is the way it's been for me." He shook his head. "I don't get a second chance."

&.

The ferry to L'Estaque pushed out in the direction of the sea, sloshing, like a child's boot kicking into lake water. The ferry's wake unsettled a sailboat that was on its way in. The sailboat's two sailors, a man and a woman, were taking down the mainsail when they saw the wake coming; as the wake hit their boat they held on to whatever they could. There were other small boats hit by the wake. The boats tipped like bath toys. A sailor in one of them shouted heatedly up at them. Harv was not familiar with the French words, and neither were the tourists on the ferry with him. The tourists, smiling, waved at the furious sailor. The tourists raised their cameras. But Harv did not. Harv was telling Bev that Russ had met a woman and had, of all things imaginable, fallen in love, the worst that could happen to a lone wolf like Russ, and so Russ had broken it off, walked away.

Bev asked, "The worst that could happen?"

"Oh no, not the worst. I can imagine worse. Anyone could. But that's the way he described it to me. The worst that could've happened."

"Was it the right thing to do? To walk away from her."

"Oh, I don't know if it was. I do think Russ needs somebody. Everybody does. But he makes his own way, and from what I know about him he always has."

"You say he fell in love with her, and they can't be together? What a shame."

They explored L'Estaque but his mind was elsewhere. When he raised the camera to shoot it was because it was what they had come to do. He looked through the lens and sometimes he saw Russ and at other times he saw a young woman forced to entertain men in a bar. Sometimes he saw the repulsive men who made her do such things, men who were bad. He took pictures of the sea and the village and the boats in the small L'Estaque port and the boats coming in and out, the ferry, and things like these that did not really interest him now. He shot more by instinct than anything. With the camera on automatic he didn't have to turn the focus or bother with settings.

He and Bev had lunch at a café table with a view of the sea. It wasn't very different than other lunches they'd had. The lunch wasn't what they looked forward to as much as the phone call home.

Alex was home when they called. She would be home for another two weeks, suspended from school for fighting. On the phone she said that she was at this moment doing her schoolwork at the kitchen table. Her assignments were delivered each day by the school principal's secretary. They'd already learned from her mother that, during this time at home, Alex was fighting girls in the alley behind the house. Alex's mother couldn't do much about it. Her mother wasn't home every day. At her job, there was a desk to sit at, there were invoices and contracts to type up. At home, there were bills to pay and a mouth to feed. And so Alex, as Harv imagined it, when Alex found herself alone in the house all she wanted to do was provoke other girls—phone calls, emails, text messages—until one of those girls showed up in the alley, and then Alex went out to fight her. But why on Earth, Bev wanted to know. She said she couldn't imagine what eleven year olds had to fight about. "Why are they behaving like boys?"

Harv said, "It's because Alex can take a punch. What more reason does she need? Well, you remember her friend Whitney. They've been close friends, haven't they? For years now. Probably since the first grade. Whitney's a small girl but has so much weight on her now that I bet she gets picked on, because little girls can be ruthless to each other. Everybody knows that's how they can be. Boys are different. We're not talking about boys. When girls don't like one of their own and there's something not right about that poor girl, they can be ruthless. Remember back when you were her age. Were the other girls or were they not as ruthless as I believe them capable of?"

Bev asked, "What are you saying, Harv?"

"I'm suggesting that Alex is protecting someone. And if that's the case let her, just let her punch the hell out of those other girls." Harv got so mad about it he had to stand up and walk away and stand for a long moment staring at the sea.

When he came back to the table Bev said, "What's got into you, Harv?"

"Nothing. It just occurs to me that Alex has got some goodness in her and maybe nobody realizes it. She's got tenderness but has no idea how to express it. Nobody understands her like we do, Bev."

"I'm not sure I do but if you say so I'll take you on your word."

"I mean it, Bev. There's good to be done yet in this world."

"Eat your fish, Harv." Bev put an elbow on the table and looked out at the boats. "She's got two more weeks at home."

"You're thinking what I'm thinking, right?"

"I never know if I am or not which keeps me loving you."

Harv looked briefly out at the boats too, in the direction they had come, in the direction of the old port, where there was their room at the hotel, their luggage and the other small things they had brought with them. "We've got to get back," he said. "We'll stay with Alex during the days. So she won't have to be alone. We'll talk to her and get at the root of this and we'll help her through it. We should get our papers from the consulate tomorrow and then at least in my mind we're as good as gone. We're getting on a plane."

Her eyes were wet and she was squeezing his arm. "Yes, Harv. Yes, we're going home."

It was such a relief to hear her say this in the way that she did. He could tell she meant it. He took her hands in his and then they leaned in and held each other.

18

Noémie

I n late morning, a morning that was already too hot, Noémie for no other purpose than to buy bread entered the Place Notre-Dame Du Mont from rue Fontange, toward the cafés, the bakery, and the market stand where she might today also buy strawberries and radish.

She often walked on this street of the La Plaine quarter. She knew it well. Every so often she bought bread from this bakery on the Place Notre-Dame Du Mont. This Place was named after the old church Notre-Dame du Mont that stood with a bell tower. This was the church where in the 16th century Frederic Chopin played organ at a funeral. Noémie called it the church of sad music. Along the edge of the Place, cars and trucks of all shapes and sizes passed on rue de Lodi on their way to and from Ailleurs, and parked along the sides of the street.

On the Place, people of the quarter took respite at café tables under umbrellas. Big red, brown, and blue umbrellas stood open under the Marseille hot sun like a lawn of colored mushroom caps, the people under them like bugs. The bright red of La Terrasse Bataille, the brown of the Café Le Petit Montmartre, the bright blue of the Bar du Marché. Pigeons flapped their wings on tree branches above a taxi lane, where a sign read *sauf taxis*. The old church of sad music looked over all from across the rue Fontange. Corey had told her that this Place was where he met a Monsieur Buisson to buy weed. They met behind bushes by the bakery. "Was it true?" she'd asked him. "Why not the Cours Julien square, where everyone else buys weed?" Corey had said it was safer in the Place Notre-Dame Du Mont to do such things. She said it was not safe anywhere to meet a man behind bushes. Corey agreed with this, and said it was because in the Place Notre-Dame Du Mont no one paid attention. "Only the pigeons eye you," Corey had said, "and the church."

Noémie at rue Fontange, entering the Place, turned toward the cafés, the bakery, and the market stand—then she heard a sound. It was a small sound, but when she heard it she experienced a sensation. It was as if she felt the sound, as if the sound tugged the skin of her arm. This particular sound might have gone unnoticed in the constant noise of the quarter, the sounds that rise and fall, the sounds of cars and all the people of the quarter. But not for her. For Noémie, it reached her ears. It did not go unnoticed. Others who were passing did not pause and those at the café tables did not look up. A gray cat, up in an apartment window, looked out and that was all.

Noémie heard this sound again. It was a human sound, a woman. But it was not at ease, it was sharp and brief and it may have been a cry.

There were other sounds, too, and Noémie realized that these sounds were together; it was a commotion. And it was nearby.

She stopped, to silence her own steps, to listen for the source, for this commotion was coming to her ears as nothing more than small sounds. She looked up at the apartment windows, some shuttered, some with open shutters and the paned windows standing open. The cat looked back at her. The commotion was not there. But it might have come from up there, one of those apartments, or from inside one of these cafés, or even from inside the Tabac on the corner. The sound might have come from anywhere nearby. She was compelled to listen because an instinct told her that something was indeed happening nearby, and that she must at once come to understand it. She turned around, looking, and ran her fingers under the purse strap over her shoulder to ease the weight of it, and then she pushed her hair back and then she pushed the sunglasses up into her hair, to more clearly see, while she turned around, all the way around, still turning, still looking to see what it was that was happening somewhere nearby.

A young man discovered it first. On the other side of rue de Lodi, the young man with his backpack cried out, *Connard!* with disgust, *Asshole!*

And he said it again more furiously, the word *Connard!* coming up out of his gut, and he pounded the side of a parked truck with his hand as he passed it, and then he was walking away, angry.

But what had he seen to make him say this, who was the *connard*, and why had he struck the truck in the way that he had? Noémie did not see. And then she saw, in the front window of that truck. She spotted them. It was a man and a woman.

The man was behind the wheel; the woman in the other seat, against the door. And then Noémie saw him strike her. It was like he was reaching over to the woman, but it was a violent swift movement. What else could it have been but a blow? And the woman cried out when struck, her cry muffled behind those closed doors. He was beating her.

Noémie ran across the street and pounded on the truck window where the man was inside but he was turned away and he was beating the woman and he would not stop.

Noémie ran around to the other side of the truck and pounded the window and yanked the door's handle but it was locked. She pounded the window where the woman was but the woman too was turned away, she would not respond, her head was down, she was turned inward under the force of the blows. Noémie shouted, pounding the window, "Stop! You must stop! What are you doing? Stop!"

And then, as if for Noémie, the man took the woman's head in his hands and he began to pound her head against the glass. Noémie shouted, "Stop!" But he would not. Noémie looked desperately for someone to help. Where had that young man gone? How could he have walked away? She shouted, as she fumbled for the phone in her purse, "Police! I'm calling police!"

The man again pounded her head against the glass, and then Noémie screamed at the sight of the woman's blood on the window.

Noémie dialed the phone with shaking hands.

And then, as suddenly, he stopped. Noémie's eyes locked with his. She could see into the very core of him in this instant, and she could see the primitive of him, the loathsome ancient savage.

Probably he saw nothing but the phone in her hand. Noémie could not know. Probably he'd realized that she was calling the police, probably he felt a fear of being arrested. Certainly it was this fear that made him withdraw from the woman. He turned away from where the woman lay against the door with her face on the window, her eyes closed, her mouth open, blood and saliva on the glass. Certainly it was base fear that made him start the truck. Probably he felt nothing else now. Probably now he was empty of everything but fear. A man with nothing inside him except all that was animal: blood and bones, and flesh enough. Maybe he was an undocumented immigrant, and if caught would receive the *double peine* of jail time and then expulsion. Maybe this was the fear in him. As such, he could not see in Noémie's eyes all that he was not, all that he could not be, and the truth of how base he was.

Noémie said to the woman, "Open the door!"

And she pounded the door and yanked at the handle: "Open the door!"

But the woman's eyes were not open. She did not move.

Noémie pounded the door: "Get out! Come with me!"

The man spun the tires, lurched the truck into the street, and sped away. Noémie repeated the truck's registration plate to the police on the phone, saying slowly, "BC," and "831," and "HT." She repeated these numbers again and again to make sure the police had it right, to make sure they were going to find the truck and rescue the woman. The absolute accuracy of these numbers was all that might save her from him.

The police asked her for the plate numbers. She repeated them again.

"It was a van?"

"No," she said, "it was a truck."

The police asked, "Was she a prostitute?"

The question sent a shudder through her. She grew furious with them, shouting into the phone: "She was not a prostitute! It was not a van. It was a truck. The man and woman were of the same place. It was evident in the skin. What does it matter? It shouldn't matter. Why do you ask? No, she wasn't a prostitute. Do you have the numbers now? You must find him and take him. He might be a father. If you won't think of the woman, think of their children."

The police were silent on the phone now.

Noémie said, "Hello? Are you there? Repeat it to me. I need to hear you repeat the truck's numbers. We must check the numbers again for accuracy, to make sure you have them. She's dying there with him. You must find her."

The police were silent.

"Hello? Are you there? I will call the newspapers. They will tell the world what you have failed to do."

The line disconnected.

She stood in the empty place where the truck had been. She looked around. No one was there to help. She called the police again. They said they'd made the report and were already investigating and looking for the truck. She did not believe them. They hung up on her. She went home.

How to reach William at the *New York Times*? He would listen to her. This was important and no one was listening to her. Not just this matter, but all of these, all of these were matters of life or death. But she could not call William on the phone. It was just what he did not want, because if she called him then someone might discover. Their affair, four years ago, had not been so long ago, though certainly a life event behind her, a thing of the past. It had happened in the brief time between Montreal and Marseille that she'd spent living with friends in New York. If she called his cell phone, his wife might pick up. The wife had never suspected him of doing the things he'd done with Noémie. The wife was the same woman he'd said he would leave though he never did. Thank goodness he hadn't left his wife, because William was not the man for Noémie. They were too different. It was not enough to say that they were too different but these words were easier for her than other truths. Their sex had been amazing. Their sex had been out of this world. The best she'd ever had. But in everyday things they did not negotiate, they did not work out compromises. They argued. He was stubborn, needing everyday things to be done his way, one way only. Somehow, their fights had fulfilled a need for him. Sometimes the arguments had been fierce. Sometimes he got so angry he punched a wall or a pillow but he had never hit her. The instinct for violence was in him like it was in every man but he had good control of it. In that way, for Noémie, he was a better man than most other men.

She wrote a letter to him at his office. His office was in midtown Manhattan, in a skyscraper on Avenue of the Americas. She'd visited his office once but he would not see her there, not in the way that she wanted, though she had tried to pull off his clothes. She'd tried to do all that in his office because there was such risk and always it was the element of risk that made for hot sex, and she'd understood this but he wasn't willing to do it there, he wouldn't close his office door, he wouldn't let her pull off his clothes.

Noémie wrote to William and some of the anger seeped in that had become their way of being together at the end. She wrote that he must send a journalist to Marseille.

She sealed it, but she had more to say. She picked up the pen again and wrote him a second letter asking him to call her, so that she could explain better the urgency of sending a journalist to Marseille, because it was too much to write in a letter, it would be easier to tell him all of it on the phone. She wrote a third letter.

But he never called.

PART TWO

Julio

Had something happened to Julio on the road up to the church under the hot Marseille sun, thousands of miles away but not so long ago, a few weeks ago, Julio's shirt heavy with sweat, the backpack of camera gear too much of a burden, and the notebooks, the papers, the map, the guidebook, even the coins in his pocket, even the wristwatch, all of this equipment too much to bear? The batteries, the lenses, the camera stand, the breakaway microphone, the portable light, its power pack, its tripod stand, the clothespins, the reflectors, the laptop and its external drives?

Place him now at the end of a long yard with New York City's East Village low-rise buildings up in front of the sky, with none of his equipment, on a bench with his shoes off, an early summer green lawn under his feet. It was an enclosed lawn, within a mortared stone wall. He squeezed grass with his toes. It was the Marble Cemetery, a cemetery without headstones, behind an iron gate on Second Avenue. Open to the public a few days each year and today was one of the days. This intimate green space was out of the way, an aside. By most, it went unnoticed. A space of plush lawn and flowering bushes, and marble plaques up on the surrounding walls to mark vaults below ground. Julio on a bench regarded the wall and its marble plaques. He did not know what was happening inside his head, it might be medical, it might be mental, he didn't know what it might be, but it was evident to him that a peculiar and anomalous thing was happening. He remembered what he'd done earlier in the day at home. He'd erased the video files, and torn his field notes into shreds along with the map of Marseille, that French port city so far away with its church on a hill.

He'd crawled out the apartment window and burned the paper shreds. He'd burned them because he was good at piecing things together, puzzles, camera equipment, stories. It wasn't only his training as a journalist, all of his life he'd had a real knack for this. And so, to keep himself away, he'd had to burn them. He stuffed the shreds in a paper bag and crawled out the window to the fire escape. He went up onto the roof, climbing the fire escape up two floors, past windows of neighbors who may or may not have been home. The roof was gray and black with fiberglass and asphalt treatments, and seals and flashing, and pipes, cables, and a chimney, and some trash of cigarette butts and beer bottle caps. All around, a bleak terrain of rooftops and ill-assorted buildings and the high smokestacks of the power plant on the East River. It was hot up there, with a late morning sun. There were some gusts of warm wind so it took six or seven matches to get the fire going. And then after some time even though the shreds had burned enough he stood watching it and its smoke. Abruptly a gust shot away what was left of the bag, blowing it over the edge. He climbed down the fire escape and back through the window.

Now in the Marble Cemetery, he remembered all of that clearly. Amy his wife of five years crossed the lawn—he hadn't seen her come through the iron gates from the narrow alleyway, but here she was crossing the lawn to him—and she sat on the bench beside him, leaning forward with elbows on her knees and fingers knitted together, regarding the same stone wall and its marble plaques he'd been regarding now for some time. He said, "You found me." He'd left her plenty of clues. She seemed too upset to look at him, but then she put her arms around him. She was warm. It was a warm place to be, in her embrace. And when she withdrew he watched her, knowing that she could not reconcile what he had done and that she wanted to ask questions but didn't know where to begin.

He said, "Do we begin with language?"

"What else is there?"

"Do you trust me? Do you know that I love you?"

"Yes," and she seemed to wait for more, to want to understand why he would ask such questions. And then she asked, "Are you questioning this?"

He shook his head. He was having some trouble breathing. His chest was tight, but it wasn't a respiratory event or a cardiac event, it was nerves, it was only that the skin of his chest was so taut that he had some trouble pulling in each breath, but of course he was breathing, his head was paying attention to each breath. He was glad to be in an open space. He said, "I don't know when it started."

"This morning?"

"After you left for work, I was going to call you, I had the phone in my hand, the phone was there, the phone was working, but I wasn't making sense. I could say some things but I wasn't well, I couldn't speak well, you see. And I didn't recognize some of the words. It's like someone else was talking. I was trying to say things, but someone else was speaking and so I was trying to talk over that person but that person was me."

"What triggered this? Did you meet with someone this morning? Did you read something?"

"No, I think it started much earlier. Not days. Weeks or months or years. I don't know."

"Did something happen to you in Marseille?" Her questions went on like this, desperately. He told her that this was the first time he'd ever had an attack like this, if attack was the right word. They talked about an episode that had happened to him in Haiti, a year ago, but he felt that that was not the same, and that that was not to blame for this. She looked for something or someone to blame—had someone made him do this?—but there was no one.

She kept trying to understand it. "Is it something medical? Have you had a stroke?"

"No, I don't believe so."

"Let's get you to a doctor."

"What would I say to a doctor? I can't describe this. I won't have answers. The doctors will want to do tests but they'll find nothing wrong."

"I was afraid you were hiding something medical from me. Are you?"

"What would I hide?"

She exhaled a short fearful laugh: "Cancer? I don't know. Something else? Something that will take you from me?"

He shook his head.

She said, "I can't help but think that the work you did in Port-au-Prince and the tent cities must have something to do with this."

"That was more than a year ago."

"Then what happened in Marseille? Was it really so bad? What was bad about Marseille? Did someone hurt you there? I've never seen you like this. You destroyed your work. You wrecked the desk at home. You wrecked the room. It's like a hurricane came through. The window was open. I thought you'd—I don't know what overcame you. But of course I've never seen you like this. This is something new. I wish you'd never gone anywhere. Let someone else go to those places. I watch you leave and then I'm here without you and then you come back like this. Now it's like a piece of you has died and you're still carrying it around. A dead weight. A weight that's sad and tragic and awful to carry around with you. But maybe this isn't at all what's happening to you. It's you, not me—I can't really know what's happening to you, and you can't expect me to."

"I don't expect you to."

Before them, on the wall, a stack of three marble plaques to mark the graves. The highest plaque read:

HENRY FANNING.
JOHN STEARNS.
ADOLPHUS LANE.
VAULT
No. 66.

"Just get to it," she said. "So we can know how to treat it. Keep going at it. Assemble the facts. Put the story together. Get at the truth of it. That's what you do best. It's your training. It's more than that, it's your nature. At least, it's been your nature, as I understand it. It's a part of you I fell in love with."

"I didn't feel it coming."

"You've been different. The past few days. Weeks maybe. Since you came back from Marseille."

"Different how?"

"You stopped asking questions."

"Oh I see. That's what you mean when you say it's like a piece of me has died."

"It's who you are. You always look for answers."

"I was up on the roof. I went up the fire escape. Burned some notes. When I came back down the fire escape, I leaned out over the rail. I looked down into that distance, and I asked myself if it was high enough to do the job and if it was really the best way. But I shouldn't be telling you this. Let me just add that I wasn't setting out to do that. I wouldn't do that to you. I wouldn't leave you like that, and I hope you know that I wouldn't. I'm not trying to worry you that what I'm thinking about is how to end my life. I was only looking for answers. I only tell you this because I was looking for answers."

"That's fantastic," she said, her eyes widening. "Really it's the best news." She chewed her lip, as if she didn't want to say what she was thinking. "As long as you do that, and I mean as long as you keep asking questions, then I'd say you're in good shape."

"Oh good. I'm glad to hear it." He knew she was trying to talk him out of this. She would say anything. Anything might help. He couldn't know.

She said, "After Haiti, the doctor, do you remember what he said? He told you to talk through all of it. Write it down, whatever it takes. To help you remember what happened. So listen to him. Talk about this. Do you want to talk about Marseille?"

He shook his head. "I don't know what I would talk about."

Her lips were red, parted; he could see her teeth, the same color as some of those old stones of the wall. Words were coming from behind those stones. He regarded the wall again as she talked. He squeezed grass with his toes. She tried to pull him away from the marble cemetery, to take him home, but he wasn't ready to leave. She said, At least let's go to one of the cafes, one of our regular spots? Have a cold drink, have a sandwich, a basket of chips, anything, somewhere that was away from this depressing cemetery and where there would be the city bustle and they might even see friends. But no, he could not leave. He needed to be out in the open. He was fixed to the place and he did not know why it was impossible to leave, only he could not. She left and came back with paper and pens. She put a pen in his hand. He said, "I bought this pen in Marseille, on rue Fontange." She took it from him and put another pen in his hand. But he gently took the pen from Marseille back from her and held onto it. She asked if he would like her to bring his video camera, if it might be easier for him to talk to the camera. He shook his head. He took up paper and the pen from Marseille but felt that he had nothing to write. When she left, he was alone again.

Some time later, Bill, his editor, arrived and sat with him on the bench. It was a surprise. He'd never seen Bill outside the office. Amy must've asked him to come. How much had she told him? And while smoking, which wasn't allowed in the Marble Cemetery as everyone knew, Bill too regarded the wall and the marble plaques. The middle one read a name that was illegible, with the first letter J:

J—
VAULT
No. 117.

The lower one could not be read, the engraved name and vault number effaced over such an expanse of time, Julio could not know how long it had been, possibly a hundred and fifty years, possibly two hundred.

Bill said, "I don't understand."

"You mean what's on the wall? Those are markers."

"What is this place?"

"It's a cemetery, one of the oldest in Manhattan. Instead of graves with headstones, there are underground vaults. I've asked these questions. There are marble rooms, vaults, hollows, that we can't see under us, ten feet under the grass here. The markers have the family name and the location of the vault underground. There are only markers on the surface, up on this wall, that we can see."

"What do you think of that?" Bill was leaned forward, one elbow on a knee, his head turned to look him straight in the eye.

Julio couldn't stand to be looked at this way. Because Bill would try but wouldn't be able to figure out what had happened. Bill was the editor. He was good at polishing a rough story and good with the budget for stories, but not so good with the work of digging for pieces and fitting these together. Bill had once been a reporter but not for long, and it had been too long ago. Julio said, "I understand it's a grid down there deep, under the grass, of marble vaults six columns by twenty-six rows. There are something like two thousand people buried here. It's a half acre of land. The first was a child. Most of the early ones were children."

"What a cheery place. What do you think of it?"

"I think it's not enough information somehow."

"You'd like to see more of the story. Can't put it together?"

"I don't know what I'd like to see. Maybe nothing at all."

"You've seen too much, is that it? Stop me when I'm wrong. The work in Haiti was rough on you. A rough spot for anyone. It doesn't mean you weren't the best person for it. I'm trying to say the right thing. What do you need to hear? Let me be blunt. You need to tell me when you're not up for an assignment. I mean before you take it. This doesn't look so good on me either."

"I don't know that this has anything to do with Haiti."

"Of course it has to do with Haiti. That's when it started, isn't it? You gave up. We had to pull you out."

"I know you did."

"I sent you to Haiti to get at what was really going on there. Now Marseille, that was just about the same job. Because the EU pinned a ribbon on Marseille. They gave it first place, the big award, a European capital of culture. Wow, goddamn, how about that? Did you hear that? They pinned a ribbon on Marseille. Did you know I get letters? I get letters. What a wonder that is. People get so moved by our work that they sit down and write me a goddamn letter. They take time out of their day to let me know a thing or two. I even get letters from Marseille. Imagine that. So you are feet on the ground for me. I need video. I need story. A look into what's really going on. The crime. The corruption. The poverty. The Muslim tension. Racial tensions. Everything. What it's like today and what's coming. So what went wrong? Help me understand what happened to you."

Julio could not. Haiti had been different. He hadn't prepared well enough, not in his head. That's how he'd come to understand it. Before leaving for Haiti he'd conferred with others who'd been there. Research and preparation were part of the job. He'd done those by the book, so he'd known what to expect—except that he had not known what to expect. Nothing by the book could have prepared him. Having been brought up in a small town, whether it was the small town or the humble beginnings or what, he could not say, but something about how he'd been put together as a person had made it impossible for him to reconcile the Haitian suffering under poverty and the deaths. But Haiti had been more than a year ago, and its effect on him had not been the same as the attack, or fit, he'd had today. Or was it only the symptoms that were different? He felt that he could not know, not with the few facts at hand. He didn't understand what had made him do what he did to his video files from Marseille, the notes, all the papers, everything. He couldn't help Bill understand.

Bill said, "You've been pummeled, haven't you, by all that you've seen? First hand contact with poverty really gets at you for some reason. Sinks its claws into you. You're soft. It gets at nobody else quite like it gets at you. Maybe you're too soft for this work. Anybody ever tell you that?"

"No," said Julio. "Only you say such things."

"Want to hear more? You're not listening."

"I'm listening. I'm here."

"Well," Bill said, dropping his cigarette on the grass and pressing it out with his shoe, "to begin with, two thousand people buried here."

"Two thousand stories. The two thousand stories aren't here. They didn't start here."

"Good to hear you say that. But it's two thousand and one. You're missing the big story that frames the place and pulls it all together."

Julio didn't say anything to this. Bill was right. He didn't feel that he needed to agree or disagree with Bill. He wanted Bill to leave. And then Bill was quiet. Julio had the sense that Bill would stand up and leave, but he didn't, not yet. Bill said, "Amy says you wiped out all your material. Was it everything from Marseille? What have we lost? Everything? I should make you choose your own replacement. I should give you that pain. It's painful to assign someone who isn't right for it. But I don't want to do that. I don't want to replace you. You can still speak French, can't you? Or have you lost that, too? My guess is you can still do the work. Stop me when I'm wrong. And anyway I don't want to pay for someone else to start over from scratch. All of it's still in your head, right? Stop me when I'm wrong." Julio felt Bill's stare for some time, and then Bill left. Alone again, Julio squeezed grass between his toes, Julio regarded the wall and its marble plaques.

&a

After this peculiar fit happened to Julio, landing him for a day on a bench in the Marble Cemetery, it was easy to clean up the room with the desk in their East Village apartment, and get back to work. It was easy to put everything back on the desk: the pens and pencils, notepads, magazine clippings, the scissors, the stapler. It was easy to pick up the desk's spilled drawers and push them back into place. It was easy to sweep up the paper shreds, to right things, to stand up the magazine rack by the sofa and the trash bin at the desk, to stand up the chair, to re-shelve the books, to wipe clean his footprints from the windowsill at the fire escape. It was not an event of great significance because no story had been lost. All the Marseille research that he'd destroyed had not yet become a narrative. Pieces had not been put together.

Amy feared that he'd had a stroke. Julio went to a doctor, who found nothing wrong with him, so the doctor sent Julio to other doctors. More tests were run. Nothing unusual was found. Julio was experiencing no symptoms now. He hadn't experienced a symptom since that day. It was agreed that he'd made a complete recovery.

At the office, he didn't want his colleagues to know that he'd experienced a peculiar fit, but word got around and questions were asked. His colleagues were journalists and this was their training. But there wasn't much substance to the story of what had happened to him, what he'd done, why he'd done it. It wasn't really very interesting. Everyone knew the work was hazardous. One needed a break between assignments. Some colleagues suggested that something born of Marseille's filth had infected Julio, probably something brought up from North Africa or over from one of the islands or down from festering farmlands. A colleague even suggested a correlation to the PTSD of soldiers, but this was not nearly as interesting an angle as a soldier's PTSD experience, a far more compelling narrative. So the questions stopped, and for Julio in very little time things returned to normal.

ॐ

A month later Julio returned to Marseille on orders from Bill to finish the assignment, and was well into the research work when it happened again. He felt like a jammed camera, as if the intricate machinery inside of him wouldn't go into gear, some notched wheel wouldn't turn, the shutter would not open, in this peculiar fit, and so it was impossible go on with the work.

Julio dialed into the newspaper's exchange to place an international call from France, and he called Amy. With much static on the line, there was only her voicemail. He checked his watch. It had three faces, one of which was always on home time, New York City. The third he'd never set, and supposed it to be the watch's home country time, still on the time set by a watch factory worker. Amy in New York at this time of the morning would be on the subway heading to the midtown office building where she would take the elevator to the eighth floor. They worked at the same place but in unrelated departments. On the seventh floor was his own office, a cubicle, along with the rest of his department and his editor Bill. When Amy arrived on the eighth floor she would go through glass doors and carpeted halls to her office where there was a green avocado plant in the window with a view of the next building's glass façade, and there were books everywhere, pads of paper, pens and pencils stuck in a small tube-shaped pitcher, and a clock with two faces, one of which she kept set to wherever in the world Julio happened to be.

At least this is how Julio remembered her office to be, for he hadn't been to her office for some time. There was no reason why he hadn't, only he'd been on the road a lot and they'd both been busy, probably it had been some months since he'd been to her office, maybe half a year or more.

He checked his watch again. Amy would now be on the subway with no cell phone coverage. He left her a voicemail. He said that he was experiencing something again. He was having symptoms. He tried to explain.

In saying these things, he was having trouble breathing. Some of his words were gasps. He could not speak well. He was sweating. It was just like before. And so he knew that he didn't have to tell her, he didn't have to go on about it at length, because she would know at once from the sound of him that he was having a fit. And so, he knew, she would begin to look for clues. He told her in the voicemail that he would leave Marseille immediately for Paris. He said simply a name: *Flaubert*. It's all he could manage to say now because the memory of that garden in Paris was rising in his chest the way a wave swells as it approaches shore. A wave swells because the landscape has changed beneath it. Flaubert would be enough of a clue for her. She would remember this place, too, and she would know to find him there. She would remember the Paris garden with Flaubert.

When he got off the phone he erased the video files, all that he'd shot in and around Marseille. He could not access the roof. He could not burn papers the way he had at home. Instead he tore pages of notes into shreds, separating these into three piles so that they could not be found, or recovered, in one place. One of these piles he threw out the window and the pieces fluttered down on the graffiti-covered rue Carnot. A woman out there gasped under this strange snowfall. She was walking a dachshund. He had not seen her, or he would not have thrown the pile of shreds in the careless way that he had. Her dachshund yipped, up on his back legs at the end of the leash. "Chinelo," she scolded, tugging the leash. Julio at the window saw that she saw him. What would she do? She only stared back at him. She was not angry. He expected her to be furious. But she was not. He waved to her, a sort of greeting, a sort of acknowledgement that he had done this thing to her. Paper shreds were in her hair. She had paper all over her. He called out that he was sorry. He said it in English. He said, "I'm leaving Marseille. I'm leaving." He was so worried about his state of mind that he did not really know what he was saying. She was only looking up at him. He could not read her, but he believed that she wanted to say something to him. She would not be satisfied until she said something. She might call up to him when he turned away. But she did not. He withdrew from the window. The woman went out of his head. The other two piles he divided in separate trash bins. It was then, he felt reassured, that the notes could not be recovered— that is, that he would not be able to recover the notes.

On his way out, with his bags, Julio took a moment's pause to steel himself, for he could not know what effect Marseille would have on him during the walk to the train station. He didn't know if the sight or experience of something here had triggered this fit, and would now on this walk out of Marseille stab deeper into him. The fit was upon him. It was in his head but at moments he could feel it physically, too.

It felt like bees were loose inside of him, at a hum, fairly quiet now, but might with the slightest provocation begin to swarm.

Julio rolled his bags through the Cours Julien square. It was mid or late afternoon, the sun hot. People were out and as he passed them he kept his head down. He did not know if they saw in his face or in his carriage that he was experiencing a peculiar fit. A woman caught up to him. It was the same woman. Paper shreds were in her hair. The dog was no longer with her. She said, "I live here, upstairs."

Upstairs made no sense to him. He said, "Okay." It was all that he could say. It was a moment before it occurred to him that she'd spoken English. He had nothing to say. He was worried. He began to walk away.

"Wait," she said, keeping up with him. "Take this." It was a roll of paper tied with string. "I want you to have it."

"Why?"

She made him stop. She pushed the paper into an outer pocket of the suitcase. "It's a gift. For what you did for me. A gift in exchange for what you did. I am from Canada. What you did—"

"I didn't know, I don't know why I did it, I'm sorry, I didn't know you were—"

"It changed something for me." Her face lit up. "It felt like home. I never thought it would snow in Marseille. It made me feel young again. Like I'm in a happy home. It made this place home for me. This is my home."

"I can't accept—"

"Thank you," she said, and rapidly kissed him on one cheek and then the other. Her eyes were wet. She squeezed his arm. It was as if she didn't want to let him go, but he had to go, he had to get out of Marseille.

He rolled past street kids on the low wall of the square, past the Le Même café where he had taken coffee and tartine buerre in the mornings, and the café owner Nicolas who smoked at the café door, past the fountain, with no further effect on him, and from there along some streets, down a hill, to the old quarter's artery, the boulevard La Canebière, where at the busy corner he stopped to wait for the light to cross. He felt no different here but didn't know what to believe. Several men who looked to be from North Africa, but might be from anywhere, stood looking in to watch a football match on the café's TV. To sit at one of the tables, one had to order something or at least pay a euro to sit for some time. Instead of this, they followed the match from the door. Julio didn't look to see who might be playing, he didn't ask any of the men about the match,

141

which he might've done if not for the fit that he was experiencing. Julio crossed La Canebière with the light and walked the few blocks from there to the great high steps of the train station, Gare Saint-Charles, where he heard a peal of church bells that made him anxious about the time and missing a train and missing the opportunity to get out of Marseille, to get to Paris straight away, and by the time he'd climbed up the hundred and four steps under the searing sun with his bags in tow he was out of breath, his shirt wet with sweat, his heart pounding against its walls in his chest.

In the station Julio bought a ticket for the next train to Paris and pressed through a crowd of people arriving, who were tourists, some American but there were other nationalities, too. Inside the car, the wagon as the French called it, he stored his luggage on the rack inside the car and he took his assigned seat at the window next to a man reading a book. He was thankful to have a window and to stare out at open space on the other side of it because when he looked around at the interior it seemed so small that there might not be enough air for everyone. Julio didn't even look at the man next to him, he didn't even see what was out the window, not really, only seven military officers in uniform with their bags on their shoulders, the group of them moving past on the platform to another train, to be stationed somewhere, to see action somewhere, probably in one of the West African missions. He couldn't know. He observed without curiosity. Julio's heart still pounded. He felt afraid, of what he did not know, certainly not of the military officers or of the journey itself, this journey from Marseille to Paris. In part it was a fear that there was something very much wrong with him now. It could be a medical problem, or soon would be, something awful with a deteriorating condition, even degenerative, and there would be very little time left, and what little time remained would be of suffering. It could be. Or it could be nothing. At the window, he considered that all of it could be explained away. Only he did not have any pieces that fit together into an explanation. But still, maybe it had nothing to do with him. Maybe it was only that he was feeling residual sensations of some external event. He then experienced terrible premonitions: something had happened to his brother or one of his sisters. There was no reason to believe that something had happened to one of them.

In Paris, from the train station Gare du Nord he walked to the Port l'Arsenal and on the foot bridge that spanned it he did not stop, which he might've done if not for the fit, to regard the little boats moored on the canal and a covered boat like a little ferry boat coming through, probably it was a ferry boat up to the 19th arrondissement. A political march was underway up one side of the port—he didn't see it, not really, it wasn't important—a march up to a rally at the Place Bastille. He had to get to the hotel.

Julio made his way through the streets to the hotel where the newspaper always put up its staff, and from there he sent a message to his older brother and his two younger sisters to make sure they were all right, that nothing unexpected had happened to them or any of their children, his nieces and nephews, to make sure that he had not lost someone in his life, and in messages back he was relieved to learn that everyone was all right. He was helpless. He could not piece the facts together. There were few facts at hand. Chiefly, something peculiar was happening to him. His brother and sisters were all concerned about him. They wanted to know why he'd sent such an urgent and ominous message. In as few words as possible he tried to allay their concern. He tried to explain that it was only that he'd experienced a premonition that something had happened, and of course it was unreasonable to expect that something had, because everyone was all right, nothing had happened. Otherwise he could not respond, not clearly, not at length.

He left another voicemail for Amy. His words were more clear. He was lucid. He sounded better. He felt all right. But was he? He felt a hum but here it seemed a low vibration of the city. In the voicemail he gave Amy another clue to the same garden, the place where she would find him. And as he left this on her voicemail he remembered how, on their honeymoon, years ago now, the shade of the oldest tree in Paris had given him a chill. She'd asked him, "Are you cold? How is that possible in this heat?" She'd put her arms around him and they'd moved together this way, her arms around him, more like one person than two as they'd moved together out of the shade and into the hot sun. Paris was not his. Paris was theirs, and he would not come out of this without her at his side.

In the hotel room he seemed much better. He seemed back to his old self. He was optimistic that this fit had passed. The fit had done all that it was going to do to him and now would not return. He shaved at the bathroom sink, first filling the sink with steaming hot water and then with a brush building the lather in a cup, applying it to his face, too much of it but this was always better than not enough, clearing the fogged mirror with the hand towel, and then pulling the razor with attention to the pressure of it, for too much pressure would cut his skin. It often had in the past and so he was attentive. In the mirror as he shaved he felt that the man who emerged was certainly himself, wholly himself. In this moment it was as if the fit had truly gone from him but he remained suspicious of the man he saw in the mirror and what might be happening in the head of the man.

Julio left the hotel with the room key in his hand. In the twilight, where the hotel's restaurant tables spilled out, busy with tourists at this dinner hour, a boy with roses asked at each table if someone would buy one. The boy looked to be Indian, Pakistani, Bengali, or somewhere South Asian. No one, not one of the tourists, would buy a rose, so the boy left. On his way out the boy approached him as well—Julio in front of the hotel—and when he did Julio gave him all the coins that he had in his pockets, but he did not take a rose and he felt empty of words. He sensed vaguely that questions should be asked of the boy to get at truths, but truths of what? The questions eluded him. Curiosity eluded him. No question would come together in his head. The jumble in his head had caused a jam of things. It was as Amy had said last month: he'd stopped asking questions.

In Marseille's old port, on several occasions he'd bought a blooming lilac branch from a young Roma Gypsy girl and her mother. He'd asked them about the work of selling lilac branches and the way of life that they led. Often this was in the broad pedestrian quaysides at the belly of the port in front of the church, l'Église Saint-Ferréol les Augustins. He'd learned that one could find lilacs in bloom throughout Marseille. One only had to reach out and cut the branches. Later in the day, because the Gypsies had not kept the cuttings in water, the flowers drooped, the leaves soft and curling. He'd learned where the Gypsies camped and where they would go when the police ran them out. He'd learned that her father was a horn in the jazz band that played on the Cours Julien square during the night.

This boy selling roses. The Gypsy girl selling lilacs. And Julio in this moment reflected on the boy in Marseille who'd approached him with the dead thing in his hands. Julio was just arriving home, at the door on rue Carnot, and had the keys to his door out in his hand. The boy was one of those on the Cours Julien square, one of those street kids on the wall, among the destitute and the drug dealers, a boy of maybe thirteen, looking quite a lot like the Jeanne d'Arc at the church Les Réformés, and asking in French if Julio

144

would let him use his oven, or if Julio would cook this dead animal for them, because they were hungry. It was a dead rat. The boy had killed it by throwing it against a wall. The boy said they'd tried to make a fire but police had come. Because of the fire, the police had taken some of them away, his sister among those. At the time it was after dinner and so Julio knew that he didn't have many euros left but at once he opened his wallet. But before he gave him money he told the boy to drop the rat. He told the boy that the rat could not be eaten. The boy dropped it. Julio then emptied the few euro notes from his wallet into the boy's hands. Julio went upstairs for a dustpan to use to pick up the dead rat, but when he returned the dead rat was no longer there. He tried to find the boy, concerned for the boy's health. The boy would do this same thing again, wouldn't he? The boy would try to get what money he could from others, and then he'd eat the thing because he was hungry and he'd become ill from it, because it carried such filth. Julio could not find the boy. The boy was not among others on the Cours Julien wall or on the footbridge and steps that led into the Cours Julien from rue Estelle or on the streets around rue Carnot.

In Haiti, Julio had seen children playing on the garbage heaps. When he'd asked some men at a fire about it, the men had said the children were little hunters. Julio asked, "Hunting for what?" And they'd said, "For food. The rat. We cook the rat. We tell the children not to eat before we cook, but they are hungry."

ꝫ♠

The next day Julio knew that Amy would not arrive in Paris because it was simply too soon. He felt all right, and he thought he was better, so with a notebook and a pen he went to Café de Flore, in the 6th, at Boulevard Saint-Germain and rue St. Benoit. Amy would arrive, he believed, on the second or third day. Possibly later, on the fourth day, or the fifth. Because the way to Paris was always more complicated than one expected it to be. One spent hours trying to find a reasonable last-minute ticket. Only the late-night flights were affordable. These flights arrived the following day, in the morning in Paris. Always the packing of suitcases was not easy. Laundry had to be done. A catsitter had to be hired and the key transferred to the catsitter. Plants had to be watered, windows locked, and some pocket cash secured from the bank. Always there was work at the office to manage. Always there were deadlines to meet in advance. Because the world does not stop turning when one's spouse experiences a fit. One cannot rush out at once. He expected Amy to arrive the fourth day or maybe the fifth.

At Café de Flore, Julio went directly upstairs where it was less occupied. There were no tourists. There were some customers and these were writing important work, even scholarly, as evidenced by their notebooks of lined paper and pens and their reference books. This was an ideal place to work, to write something down on paper. He'd discovered this place to work during their earlier time in Paris, some years ago.

Julio ordered a café crème and sipped it down only halfway while he wrote for hours in the notebook all of his memories of Marseille, what he considered the most interesting experiences and even some of the everyday experiences. Some parts were easier and he wrote these quickly, words pouring out of him, filling pages, without thinking much about the words that went from his head through his hand onto the paper, while other parts like about the boy with the dead rat required moments of reflection to make sure the facts were in order, so that it would all be written straight and true. This kind of writing work was awkward for him. He was self-conscious of the form. Diary and memoir were not his forms. Whatever this form was, the content of it was all about Marseille, and as he went along he did feel in his chest and in his gut that it was important work.

After he finished, he felt more empty than ever, like he had been drained of infected fluid. He closed the notebook and went downstairs, bummed a cigarette and a light from a waiter, a monsieur, and then he smoked at the corner, feeling relieved to be out in the open again, and looking over the boulevard at the people and the passing cars and also at the parked bicycles and motor scooters nearby on the rue Saint-Benoît and also at the people out front at the tables under the awning of the nearby cafés Deux Magots and Brasserie Lipp. And then when he'd smoked some, at least more than half the cigarette, he tossed the cigarette into the street. He went back upstairs to the table where everything was as he had left it: the café crème, the notebook, the pen.

He looked back at what he'd written, and it was illegible. His immediate reaction was that something had happened to the notebook; this was not his notebook, not his writing; someone had done an exchange. He looked around at the others—they were all silent, working. What he suspected simply could not be true. It was paranoia. It was only that he was having a fit. He was deep in it. He went through the pages again. Ticks with the pen, and little swoops and crosses and curves and corners. Not a single identifiable letter of the alphabet. The text before him was not in code. It was gibberish. All of the work he'd done here amounted to nothing.

The moment was more dangerous now. He couldn't trust himself. He did not know what he might do, without knowing, without intending harm—he might even harm someone—how could he know what he might do?—and of course it was nonsense, this sensational fear of harming someone, because he'd never hurt anyone in his life, indeed he was the opposite, he was the one whom people trusted to use wits and smarts, he was not the type of man to give in to the primal instinct of a violent react. He'd never even killed an animal. His brother had. Others in his family had, while out hunting. Julio had aimed, he hadn't aimed well, and every time he fired he missed. They'd all laughed about this, while he'd savored the relief, and even joy, that so far in the span of his existence he had not taken another life.

Julio left the café and then a short time later found himself, as he'd expected to all along, on a bench at the Square René-Viviani, arriving from rue Saint-Julien-le-Pauvre, along with a peal of church bells that did not make him anxious like it had at Marseille's train station. At the Square René-Viviani, one was not surprised by the sound of bells given all the churches nearby. Here Julio found the sound of bells to be a comfort, like a sign or an indication that he'd arrived right on time.

❧

The second day, while at the Square René-Viviani, a man walked toward Julio as if to sit on the bench next to him, which took Julio by surprise because he expected no one yet, Amy would not be in Paris so soon, and also there were many benches where no one was sitting. After this moment of surprise, he recognized behind the beard the smiling face of his old friend José María. Many years ago they'd both started at the newspaper under the same photo editor. José María had since given up the camera and taken up writing. Julio stood, beaming, and clasped José María's hand and they embraced, laughing, clapping each other on the back, Julio saying, "How good it is to see you, my old friend, why are you here, haven't you been in Cairo?

"Yes, I was in Cairo," José María said.

"Amy must've told you where to find me. Why are you in Paris? Please, sit with me."

They sat together on the bench, Julio sideways, with one knee up, so that he could better see his old friend.

José María said, "I had a meeting a short time ago with the Egyptian ambassador to France at the embassy on Avenue d'Iéna, in the 16th. It was not a really far walk, and I could not miss the chance to see you."

"The ambassador?"

"It may seem impossible to you now. Imagine, if we had only known four years ago at the photo department where we would be today."

"And tomorrow?"

"Who knows where we'll be tomorrow?" José María scratched his beard. "It was eight years ago I found myself in New York City, such a big impossible city to me then. You remember your first time there, yes? The skyscrapers? The noise and the lights? And at that time I was so young, really I was, but I was ambitious. I said to myself how is such a thing even possible, how do I make it happen? And then it was some years later they gave me a chance at shooting pictures for the newspaper. That is when you and I met, there at the paper. Of course you remember. But when they hired me, I didn't know enough about taking pictures, about how to work a camera, how to do the light and the settings. I knew only the words. Shutter, aperture, ISO. But I did know how to get in front of people, in front of whatever it was that was happening. I knew how to cross the lines, to go over barricades, to put myself in it."

"Bravery."

"Foolishness. I was wreckless. Remember it was Becky who said I was wreckless. She said I was going to get myself killed. She said I had to follow the rules. There were so many of my pictures she would not accept for the paper because of the way I'd taken them."

"One has to have certain permissions, sometimes. Rights."

"She was too cautious."

"It was her job as our editor."

"You were always her favorite," said José María. Julio laughed at this, and José María added, "It's true. She never stopped you."

"Because I was not brave."

"Well, I was not a good fit for the photo department." José María looked up at the tree behind them. "This tree is falling."

"It's still standing. It has not fallen because of these—you see, these two concrete pillars are holding it up. It's the oldest tree in Paris. A locust tree, put in the ground in 1601, believe it or not, so long ago, it seems almost beyond me to comprehend, a time before our American continent's countries were founded, a time before everything we know as it is today, this tree was put in the ground by a man named Jean Robin, a botanist, an arborist, who worked for the kings of his day."

"What do you think of that?"

It was the question Bill had asked him last month in the Marble Cemetery while regarding a plaque that marked the dead. "Have you been talking to Bill?" But there was no reason José María would talk to Bill. Bill was not José María's editor. Probably José María did not even know who Bill was, had never met him. Julio looked at his friend and the light had an odd effect on him briefly, or the light had an effect on Julio's eyes, somehow, an effect on the physiology of Julio's vision, because José María began to fade from view, only slightly, certainly he became transparent not unlike a ghost. Though in the next instant José María was reflecting the light as he always had. All of this startled Julio but then, at once, he understood it to be another symptom of the fit. He remained looking at his friend for a long moment. The effect, whatever it had been, did not happen again. He said to José María, "What do I think? I think that it's not enough information. Artillery during World War II brought half of this tree down. Imagine, it was blown to pieces, and it still lives. And how did it survive the hurricane of '99 that felled so many Paris trees? And I would like to know more about Jean Robin and the garden and how these paths and the trees along these paths led to the churches. All of this I would like to know."

"It's no use," José María said. "The past isn't important. There's only what happens next."

"Why do you say that? You don't believe it."

José María shrugged.

"Oh, I see," Julio said, "of course, I should've known at once. You spoke to Amy. She called you. What did she tell you? I suppose she told you that this happened to me last month at home after some time in Marseille. And so it has happened again after returning to Marseille."

José María shrugged, and wore the old familiar smile of José María.

Julio laughed. "I see you won't admit that you spoke to Amy. Well, the most valuable tool that we have, as journalists, is our ability to assemble facts, to keep peeling away toward the core of a thing, and discern among the peelings and everything else we have what it is in the story that is important and meaningful. The tool is judgment. I believe one could make do without a good nose, if one has good judgment and, of course, the willingness to roll up one's sleeves and work up a sweat. It's possible to do meaningful work. But if judgment is impaired, for whatever reason, it is impossible to work. If we are too close to the story, or if we are drunk, we can still work but until we are sober we likely cannot produce good and true reportage."

"Are you drunk?"

"Excellent question. You haven't changed a bit. No, I'm not drunk yet. But let's watch the time so that when it's the reasonable hour we may leave this place together if I'm feeling all right."

"How are you feeling, if not all right?"

"I was just telling you. I can't trust my output. When I shaved at the hotel, I saw myself in the mirror and I could not trust that I had not already shaved. And so I cleared all the lather from my face with the towel and saw that it was true, I had not yet shaved. I needed to shave. It had been a few days. Why was I was suspicious that I had already shaved? And what if I had discovered a clean-shaven version of myself beneath the lather, with no memory of having shaved? This is how I'm feeling." He wanted to tell José María about what had happened with the work of writing at Cafe de Flores but he felt that he could not talk about it yet.

"I would be concerned, too," José María said, "and I suppose it would make me feel unwell, but I don't disagree that sometimes it's not unhealthy to take a second look. We know, as journalists, that sometimes things are not as they seem. Even in your own house. It's the essence of our work, isn't it?"

"In my own house?"

Some kids, *les gamins*, little wild ones, ran behind a white and silver football, kicking it, running after it into the center of the gardens around which there was a ring of rose bushes and a bronze fountain with water from three small stag heads, and carved droplets and human figures, a sculpture by the late Georges Jeanclos of Flaubert's story *La légende de Saint-Julien l'hospitalier*. Flaubert had written his version of this medieval tale very late in life, very near his death in 1880, though the idea of writing it came to him much earlier in life when he and Maxine du Camp came across a small statue of Saint Julien in the church of Caudebec-en-Caux. Julio and Amy had discovered all of this together on that first trip to Paris years ago. They'd read about the fountain in the guide book, and then at the nearby book shop found Flaubert's story of Saint-Julien in a copy of his *Three Tales*.

José María was saying that Spain had been unstoppable and was well on the way to taking the cup but they were tired. Brazil ranked twenty-two, but they were rested today so they would stop Spain. José María always rooted for the South Americans. Spain also had the disadvantage of missing a midfielder and a striker, both injured. The worst would be a goalless draw. Earlier the Uruguayans had been trouble, provoking cards. The Brazilian striker was known for his short temper.

They were both regarding the white hydrangeas at the perimeter, and the inner ring of yellow daffodils and red tulips, this ring of blooming beds and its two vine-covered arbors—climbing roses not yet in bloom—that led to Jeanclos's fountain, and Julio remembered the blooming lilac branches in Marseille. He told José María of these and the young Roma Gypsy girl and her mother, and also of the boy with the dead rat.

José María asked, "And did you find the boy, or the rat?"

"No, I looked everywhere for him. I was desperate to find him."

"Why were you desperate to find him?"

"What do you mean why? I was worried about him. The child was going to eat a foul dead thing."

"I mean, why were you desperate?"

"Simply out of concern," Julio said.

"Tell me more about the boy's story."

"That's it."

"That's not what I would expect from you."

"What are you saying?" Julio asked. "You're trying to get at something. Tell me."

"You were so desperate to rescue the boy, you rushed right past the story of him. His story. The story of the boy, his sister, and his friends on the painted streets of Marseille. The fire on the square to cook a rat. The police rushing in. You missed it. It seems you didn't even see the story opportunity. What a great story it might've been, an important story, the kind of work I think you would like to do. To share experiences of those who cannot possibly." And then José María said, "Neither one of us is supposed to be here in this garden. Why are you here? The coverage of the reconstruction work in Haiti was rough on you. It would be rough for anyone."

The football rolled past them and then the kids followed at once after it.

Julio said, "I don't know that it has anything to do with Haiti."

"Poorest country on our side of the world. Devastated by the twenty-ten earthquake. Over two hundred thousand killed. You know all this. It was all part of the story. Something like two million displaced, in a country of ten. The gangs and their violence in the tent cities. And then cholera hit them. This despair that you are experiencing—"

"—is it despair?—"

"Anguish then. Are you well now? I mean the cholera."

"Yes," Julio said.

"They pulled you out with it."

"They treated me there."

"And then they pulled you out. I understand it wouldn't have been a problem except you did not immediately seek treatment, though you must have recognized the symptoms. You're supposed to run like hell to the clinic. But I guess you were in no shape to run. I understand you were weak, malnourished."

On a dirt road between two villages, under a searing Haitian sun, where there was nothing but the refuse and the wild of the island, someone had seen the body. It was not uncommon. It was Haiti. With so many deaths, who hadn't, somewhere along the way, seen a body? Julio did not know who had found him, only that it was a man who had been on the road and had told a man in the next village. And then when this man from the next village came to cover the body until someone could take it away, the man found that the body was not dead, Julio was still alive.

❧

From the Square René-Viviani it was really something to watch Paris tumble into its nighttime slumber, to see and hear the tourist throngs pour from the Notre Dame cathedral into restaurants like so much water draining out of one vessel into another, as the shops shuttered, and then after it was very dark, to see and hear them pour along the Seine quays and into the cafes, and then after more time —lights were up on the boulevard and bridges and quays and some side streets but not all of them, so much light in some places that it was like daytime, though on some side streets it was so dark that it seemed dangerous to pass through and so no one did, no one passed through although it was safe, as safe as could be expected in Paris, so one avoided these shortcuts and instead took the well-lit streets even though the walk took twice the time or longer, it could be more time than expected, and then after this time, in the middle of the night, some people whether they were tourists or expats or French, whether or not they were Parisians, there were these who moved about on the boulevards, the quays, the bridges, and even the darker places, there were these who moved about alone not like real people, rather like shadows, apparitions, ghosts, like something not of that time, call them what you like, certainly like something not of that time and in fact might not even have been real to Julio from his place on a bench in the Square René-Viviani.

‌‌ *

The third day the sun was so bright that Julio's eyes ached and his head, too, this pain nauseated him, and he was alone.

The fourth day he opened his eyes, lifting his head from his chest, because she had arrived—there was Amy on the bench next to him, her wheeled suitcase standing in front of her, with her hands on his arm and then on his shoulder and then on his face and up through his hair, as she moved closer to him, embracing him on the bench.

He was suspicious that this was not Amy. It seemed too soon. She was a hallucination, he feared, for he wasn't well and it was possible that he was hallucinating. "Is it you?" he asked her. "I really need to know. I can't trust that it's really you." And he pushed her away, trying to get her hands off of him because it was possible that she was not real. "How do I know it's you? Who are you?"

She was crying then. She was such a strong person, he'd seen her cry very few times and here it deeply pained him to have caused it. With tears she said, "How can you say that? It's me. It's me."

"Of course it's you, yes, it's you." And they held each other for a long time on the bench.

He said into her hair before they let go of each other, "We've been wanting to see Paris again."

She laughed, wiping her eyes, and then she said, "This is exactly what I had in mind," with the sarcasm he adored. It made him smile.

"We'll see all of it," he said. "The Monet at l'Orangerie. The home of Victor Hugo. Everything of Picasso. We'll see all of it. The Rodin sculpture garden. The catacombs in Montparnasse. We'll go into the catacombs this time, no matter how long the line, no matter if it's raining and the line is long."

She brushed his hair with her fingers. "You're sick. And I don't know how to help you."

"You can see some of it without me if you'd like." Because he would not be able to go into an enclosed place, any kind of room, it was the same with an airplane, he wouldn't be able to go into one, he wouldn't be able to stand it.

She said that he looked very sick. He was pale. He was thin. Had he eaten? Had he been vomiting? What were the physical symptoms? Had he seen a doctor? And so on. She would get him fed, she said. She would help him get better. She asked, "What were you planning to do next?"

"I don't know. I'm going to rest for a short while."

"Here?"

"Yes, or in the Square Jean-XXIII or the Place des Vosges or more likely at some point later the more intimate square, you will remember it, the orange roses—" He stopped because he was certain that she would remember the nude Aurore among the orange roses in the center of Square Georges-Cain behind the Musee Carnavalet, and so she would find him there.

She said, "Won't you come to Deux Magots for something? Some soup? A café crème? Chocolate cake? Can I lure you there with chocolate cake? Let's get you to a café and feed you something."

"I tried to go to a café on the first day but something happened to me there so I'm not well enough yet. I'm not sure enough of myself."

"I'll need the room key."

"Oh, here it is." He told her the name of the hotel and the room number, and how to get to the hotel through the streets, but she was familiar with the hotel so she could very well have figured out all of it on her own.

She asked if he wanted pen and paper, or his video camera, if he might like to talk into the camera. He did not want anything brought to him. She didn't want to leave him there, not even for a few minutes, but he insisted that he would be all right without her, it would only be a short time without her now, nothing would happen. She didn't want to leave. She continued to try to lure him to a café but he would not go. After some time he was able to convince her to take her suitcase to the hotel. And so she left him, wiping her eyes, rolling the suitcase behind her. She would change clothes. She would find a quick coffee because she said she'd been so worried about him that she hadn't been able to sleep on the plane. She would bring him food.

When she came back, arriving from rue Saint-Julien-le-Pauvre, she brought soup and a spoon. He tried to eat some of it for her though he was afraid he would retch. There was no taste to it, and no temperature. It was as if it had been ladled up from the Seine. She said she'd gone through all of his things. She said, "You destroyed your notes again, didn't you? What is it about Marseille? How did it happen?"

He told her some of what he'd tried to write at Café de Flore about Marseille. He told her about the time in Marseille that he'd been pickpocketed. He'd lost euro notes to the Noailles quarter pickpockets. Or he'd lost the euro notes some other way. Perhaps he'd inadvertently pulled the money out of his pocket, dropping euro notes when he'd gone into his pocket for one of those things he kept in the same pocket: the Marseille map, the piece of paper on which he'd scrawled the apartment's house number and street name, or his spiral-bound notepad with its stub pencil. The euro notes might've been lost when he'd pulled something else out of his pocket, but he suspected a pickpocket. He'd seen pickpockets at work in the New York City subways and in Times Square and in other cities, like in Paris at the Louvre, sometimes one of them, sometimes two working together. The Marseille guidebook cautioned of pickpockets on the Canebière, on the shopping street rue Saint-Férréol, along the quays, in the cafes, and elsewhere, in places where tourists thronged. And so when he left the Canebière for the rue Longue des Capucins, a North African market street cramped with shops and stalls, when he moved with the crowd along the narrow rue, that's precisely when it might've happened, in and out of shops, sometimes with women in the traditional long sifsari outer garment, past mounds of spices, tubs of olives, bins of dried fruits, the bakeries, and more, the aromas of these in the air, and then in the square that is the home of the outdoor produce market, in these places he looked at the men, some in the traditional djellabahs long garment, though many of them not dressed this way, and there seemed something of a desperation visible in some faces and the way some carried themselves—he saw himself in them— and if truly there was enough of the desperate feeling inside of them then there would be the temptation to steal, not because of who they were or from where they had come but because they were all of mankind, himself included, and Julio believed desperation to lead mankind to such thoughts and acts.

But then when he had arrived at the apartment on rue Carnot, coming in through the building door with the key, flipping on the hall light's short timer, and climbing the stairs up and around to the next floor, and unlocking the apartment door with the other key, and when he pulled off the pack and poured a drink to steady himself— first some water from the tap, which he drank deeply, and then second it was late enough in the day so a splash of whiskey with ice and a pour of water in the whiskey because otherwise it would be too strong—and when he walked to the window, leaned against the balustrade, and looked down at the graffiti-covered rue Carnot, he experienced a rush of memory from earlier in the day. He remembered that he'd stuffed the euro notes one at a time in the donation box at the church Notre-Dame de la Garde. He'd put all of the money in that box. Probably he'd been delirious from the long climb up the hill under the hot sun. So that's what had happened to the euro notes. It hadn't been a pickpocket. He'd given all of it to the church.

He would tell the paper simply that the money had been lost. He would not lie. He simply would not elaborate. They would then want details. They would say, Money cannot simply disappear, not so many euros. They would say, Look at what this is in US dollars. Julio would of course tell them the truth, but only enough of the truth, what he hoped would be enough. But then they would want to know more. They would want to know why it had cost so much to access the church for his work on this assignment. They would want a receipt, something with the name and business address of the church. The receipt should itemize the costs, in euros; the paper would determine the equivalent in US dollars. They would expect a stamp or signature on the receipt. Julio would tell them that a receipt was impossible. They would then tell him to write a letter of cost justification, have it approved by his editor and then the department head. All of this would have to happen. There would be meetings together to review and approve the expense. These meetings would take place in an inner conference room, where there would be no natural light, on the 22nd floor, the finance department's floor. In the conference room Julio would explain things and then they would decide. He would tell them of the climb up the hill under the hot sun. He would tell them of the equipment that he'd carried up to this church, the good mother that everyone could see from everywhere in Marseille. If luck was on his side, they would stop asking questions. He'd tell them that he'd been able to access every corner of the church. He'd filmed in the crypt and in the nave. He'd filmed the small wooden ships suspended by string high above the pews. He'd filmed the people praying.

It was later in the day now and he could see in Amy's eyes that she was tired, feeling the time difference, because it was the middle of the night back home in New York City. And the work to try to understand him had exhausted her. He said that she should get some rest and that he would join her later at the hotel. He would join her after a little more time. He told her that she did not need to wait there with him in the Square René-Viviani. And so she went to the hotel to rest. He'd said all that but he knew that he would require more than, as he'd said, a little more time. Not any time soon could he return to the hotel. He needed to be out in the open. If he did sleep these nights on these Paris garden benches, he was not aware of it.

In the middle of the night, José María came to see him, having found him in the Marais district at the Square Georges-Cain. Amy must've told him where he might be found.

At once Julio despaired to his friend, "Aurore is gone. They've taken her away."

José María said, eyebrows raised, "What is this?"

"The bronze of Aurore, the lovely nude. Here in this garden, she was there, in the center with the roses. She's gone now, but where have they taken her? It's dreadful. They have extracted the life blood from this place. Haven't you seen her at night, with the lights upon her, the way she shines like silver among the orange roses? When they return her, if they ever do, you must see it, José María. You must come here in the middle of the night to see her."

"Why would they take her away?"

"I have no idea. They've lost their minds."

José María said, "Why destroy the notes? All of your research? Are you hiding something?"

"You know about this?" Julio didn't know what to say to his friend.

José María continued, "Have you left any of it behind? Somewhere hidden, with a plan to go back for it? No? I can see that no, it is not this way. You have left not a trace. You have, in fact, tried to erase yourself from that place. In Marseille, you did not belong in the picture. It is the same with Haiti, and all the other foreign locations they've sent you over the years. But that is understood. It is our work to go where we do not belong. I believe I taught you that."

"By example," Julio said. "And you taught me that the core of our work is not in the craft of a newspaper story, or the crop of its photos or the cut of its video clip. It is in the chase of it. The pursuit of its facts. I used to think of us as writers. But we're not, it's not at all the same work."

"I taught you this?" He chuckled. "No, you were taught this the first time you were hurt in the line of our work."

They went on talking like this, examining the shape and aim of their work, holding it under a light so to speak, just like the old days together in New York City, at Jimmy's Corner in Times Square, or wherever it was convenient, the place was not so important, countless hours spent together, and it was not long before daylight.

Julio could smell his friend. This occurred to him vaguely at first but then he took cautious notice because he'd learned to distrust himself. The smell was something of a church, the Roman Catholic church of his childhood and probably of José María's childhood as well, an incense, something of burning coal wafted from a thurible, the single chain metal censer of burning incense. Julio said, "I can smell you. Where have you been?" And then he remembered Cairo. José María had been in Cairo, and so probably José María had been among the market stalls of Cairo's Khan el-Khalili, on the medieval lanes of the Souk es-Sudan passing through aromatic clouds of perfume and incense. Is this why José María smelled? All of this, and the company of an old friend, raised for Julio the childhood memory of pouring out of the station wagon at the church with his brother and sisters. And through the church doors was the vestibule. The vestibule was a small room of doors. The nave of pews was straight ahead through double doors. A door to the left was the cry room where his mother took his youngest sister Brigida when she cried and then watched Mass through its big interior window. To the right was the sacristy, a narrow room with closets and cabinets. The sacristy was where on certain Sundays, after Julio turned nine, Julio and his brother put on the cassock and surplice of altar servers and said the vesting prayers and then walked with Father Travieso out through the vestibule and into the nave and up to the altar. This ceremonial walk was the procession of the cross bearer, the altar servers shortest to tallest, the priest, and others, up to the altar.

But on many Sundays Julio sat in the pews with his mother and brother and sisters. His mother chose the pew. She led them up the center aisle and stopped them at a pew of her choice despite his older sister Teresa's remonstrations that she should be able to choose the pew, why couldn't she ever, why wasn't she allowed? Teresa was never allowed to choose, but always she went first into the pew, which made her special. Sometimes when their mother could not hear, Teresa explained to Julio that she was special, and that he was not. His mother sent Teresa in first, furthest from reach because Teresa was the most well-behaved, followed by Eduardo, and then either Brigida or Julio. Julio as everyone knew was the troublemaker.

He was restless, fluttering the daily missal and the hymnals, antagonizing his siblings, pinching Teresa's arm, wanting to wrestle Eduardo. Always Julio had to be within reach. "Settle down," his mother said to him. "Stop it," she whispered. Outside the church after Mass, people said to his mother that Julio was too much for her to handle. Julio was simply too much of a boy, the boys are more difficult, it was evident in every misdeed, some boys are impossible, they can't really be disciplined.

During this time his mother told him that he would meet with Father Travieso. It was a conference, his mother had said. The conference would be at the Father's office in the parish hall on the following Saturday. She told Julio that it was because he misbehaved, though it wasn't a punishment, it was a conference. Julio didn't understand. She said the Father would give him guidance. And he should prepare to meet with the Father. He should write down questions. He could write any questions down and she wouldn't see them. The questions would only be for the Father. And so on Saturday with a spiral notebook, a few questions written there, and a pen, Julio got in the car and his mom dropped him off at the church. He met Father Travieso in the church office in the parish hall. At once the Father growled, "What the hell is wrong with you? You don't listen to your mother. Kids these days..." and, raising his voice, "You don't know what you want, you've got no man in the house to set you straight, you've become stupid, haven't you?" The Father slammed something on his desk—Julio jumped. "Listening? Are you listening?" Julio said yes sir but the Father hadn't waited. "If there wasn't good at the heart of man I would know already that you are lost, that you are too far gone, lost at sea, overboard, and who cares that you gave up the ship because others are worth our time and attention." The Father barked at him for half an hour until, finally, "Get out of here!" and Julio with wide eyes got up from the chair and backed away, shaking, and then in the station wagon's front seat all the way home was silent, looking away out the window, hearing his mother's questions and feeling her eyes on him.

In the light of the morning, José María said, "Well, really we're nothing more than purveyors of truth."

"Noble merchants?"

"What does it matter who we are, where we come from, how we do what we do, as long as we produce meaningful work? Because to produce meaningful work we must be of good character, and so these go together, these rely on one another, in balance. The slightest tip of the scales will ruin our character and the work with it."

"How does one know, is it possible that one can know, whether one's work is meaningful?" He said this in French and José María understood.

"The work in Haiti was rough on you. It would've been the same for anyone in your place. How do we measure its value?"

"What is value? How does one know?"

"How many—" José María hesitated.

"How many what?"

"How many have been hurt in the work? How many have you hurt?"

Julio said, "But I have hurt no one."

"Haven't you?"

A short time after José María left, Amy arrived, so soon after that they might have passed each other outside the square on rue Payenne. Or maybe José María had turned left, and Amy had come instead from the other way, from the rue des Francs Bourgeois. Because evidently they had not passed each other: when Amy walked around the square's center rose bed and sat on the bench beside him, she made no indication that she'd just seen his old friend.

Julio said to her, "I never asked José María all that he meant when he told me that people could be hurt in our line of work. Not ourselves, because of course we can be hurt in our line of work, we can be pushed to the ground, shot, taken captive, killed. That is not what he was talking about. Instead it was something about hurting others, not in the obvious ways. How many have I hurt? I cannot say. I don't understand his question. But it seemed an important question to him and he seemed to have an answer."

She was watching him closely. "Why do you speak of José María?"

"I saw him last night. And the other day. Didn't I tell you?"

She furrowed her brow. It seemed there was something she wanted to say but he couldn't know what it was.

"He's been in Cairo. You must've told him where to find me."

She put the back of her hand on his forehead. "You're warm." She was so concerned, he knew it was this, that her eyes were wet now.

He said, "It's the sun. I have to stay out of the sun."

"You don't need to be talking to anyone but me, you understand? No more José María. No one else."

"Why not?"

"Just promise me."

"What if he comes—"

"No."

And so he did promise her and then when she left him for a short time he was alone.

୬

He did not really believe anything at all was wrong with talking to José María. If José María walked into the square from rue Payenne, what would he say, would he ask José María to leave the Square Georges-Cain, would he tell his friend to leave? Under this hot sun, would he tell José María to leave the shade of this square? Would he explain that he'd made a promise not to talk to him? He would tell José María that Amy had made him promise. And then why, why had Amy made him promise this? If José María asked him why, Julio would not have an answer. It seemed to be out of concern for his health. She feared that he was feverish. But the promise was irrational. The promise made no sense. He did not really believe anything at all was wrong with talking to José María. He may as well have promised to cross only the right leg over the left, never the left over the right. What was the harm?

Julio found himself on the Square Jean-XXIII on a bench with thickets of the heart-shaped leaves above him. He was under the shade of linden trees, rows of these trees shaped like big boxes, forming great hedgerows, and he was seated on a bench facing away from the center of the Square Jean-XXIII, where there stood the Fountain of the Virgin, *la Fontaine de la Vierge*, gothic-styled in a thin and high pointed arch, amid long beds of tulips, and behind all this up in the sky the Notre-Dame. He instead faced the left bank where some vendors on the Quai de Montebello had opened their stalls to sell prints, old maps, and books.

He was certain that Amy would easily find him there. This was not a secluded garden, not at all, situated as it was behind the cathedral, between the cathedral and the pont Saint-Louis, a short bridge linking the Île de la Cité with the Île Saint-Louis; to arrive from the right bank, one walked from the pont de Sully through the Île Saint-Louis by way of the rue Saint-Louis—the end of this rue opened up with café terraces on either side and, it seemed to arrive suddenly, an impressive view of the cathedral—and then one walked up and over the bridge's gentle rise and fall. He believed would arrive from this bridge and from the Île Saint-Louis Amy to find him.

But when, much later, she did arrive, he did not see from where. She sat on the bench next to him. She touched his face gently, her fingers on his jaw and he felt her fingers moving there against his skin and at times he felt, too, his jaw moving. She said, "Your lips are moving. Do you know that your lips are moving? Why the hell are your lips moving like this? Please stop it."

He said he hadn't known that his lips were moving but it might be because he'd been thinking of the prayers of his childhood: the Our Father, the Hail Mary, of course there had been these prayers, but also there had been the two or three short prayers his mother said before dinner, one after another, when they all held hands at the table, and also the prayer his mother said before backing the station wagon out of the driveway, which had been a prayer about angels on all sides of the car.

Amy asked, "Why are you thinking of prayers? Are you praying now, or only remembering the prayers?"

"I don't think I'm praying. I was just thinking, just now, I was just remembering the first time we went to Mom's for dinner. I made sure to tell you before we got there about the tradition of holding hands and saying prayers."

"You were embarrassed. The simple food. The four of you raised by a single parent."

"I was not. I didn't even understand what it was to be poor. We had a house. Mom was teaching at the school. We had enough to get by."

"You were very nervous anyway," said Amy. "I thought it was silly the things you were saying to me. In the car on the way there you told me there would be prayers before dinner and we'd all hold hands. And that I would be expected to say what I was thankful for, because it would go around the table to each of us. You were worried how I would take all this. Well, I didn't care one way or the other. I told you it didn't bother me that your mother wanted to say prayers. You were really worried about it, like to do all of this with your family was going to make me change my mind about you."

He took her hand. "That night at the table I took your hand and Mom began the prayers. I remember trying to see us through your eyes. There at the table was Teresa on my right who had driven over from Tampa to meet you. I remember you were on my left. And we hadn't had any wine yet. The wine had only just been poured for us as we sat down and I was wishing we'd already had some to calm my nerves. If Eduardo had been there, then Eduardo would've poured the wine earlier for himself and for us. But Eduardo wasn't there that first night. You didn't meet him until much later. But both Teresa and Brigida were there. It's true what you're saying. I was worried that you might change your mind about me. I remember your hand was trembling, our hands were trembling together, and I was worried about what was going through your head. I was worried about what you were seeing of us at the table. After all, at the time you and I didn't know each other very well."

Amy said, "Actually, it was your hand that was trembling."

"My hand? I remember it was yours, or ours together."

"It was your hand."

"I've always remembered that it was our hands together. A vibration occurring between us, because we were together and touching."

She shook her head. "No, it was your hand. I remember it clearly. You were so nervous, you were shaking."

He accepted that it was probably true that it had been his hand, instead of how he'd remembered it all this time, because he'd learned that he could not trust himself and this must include certain memories as well.

"Maybe it started then," Amy quickly said, "at that time, since you've been thinking about it, or sometime before then, but in that moment it was happening to you. During the prayers."

Julio said this was insightful of her, and that some part of what she was saying may be true, but how could he know what to believe to be true? How could she know? In the pursuit of story one must not too quickly jump to conclusions. Of course hypotheses should be made and then tested against the set of facts at hand. It is true, hypotheses should direct one's research. But it is essential to allow the story to emerge from the research rather than to shape the research to a story, and this was, he believed, something at the heart of his work. This was some of what he'd been talking to José María about.

She said she was not interested in his work. She was interested in his health. She was interested in his mind and the way his mind had been working. She was angry: "I told you not to mention José María."

"You told me not to talk to him. If you like, I won't speak of him now but he's an old friend and he's part of my life, and therefore a part of our lives, so later after all of this is over we will talk about José María and the promise."

When she left him for a short time, he was alone and during this time he hoped José María would come. He would consider breaking the promise that he'd made to Amy.

A man came into the square from along the side of the cathedral, walking toward Julio's bench, and in fact approaching Julio, but there was no beard so it was not José María, but at a distance somehow this man was vaguely familiar to Julio, this man who was walking toward him at an unhurried pace, who seemed to be heading purposefully toward him but he might simply be going through the square on his way to somewhere else. When this man came closer, under the shade of the plane trees, when Julio saw smoke from his cigarette, with a start Julio recognized his editor Bill.

Bill sat on the bench next to him and they shook hands, saying hello. It was awkward, as if many years had passed and they were meeting for a drink or for lunch to catch up on what lives they had led since knowing each other. Julio could not understand how it was possible that Bill happened to be in Paris.

Bill leaned forward, looking out at what they could see on the left bank, and said, "What's this place all about? I bet you know. Any vaults underground here?"

"I don't know about any vaults here. This was the palace and gardens of the Archbishop until the early nineteenth century. And then it was destroyed in rioting. In the flowerbeds, those are the only black tulips I've seen in Paris. They are a dark purple, very nearly black. And these trees, they are of the genus Tilia, and it was these, in Proust's Swann's Way, it was a tea of Tilia blossoms in which the narrator dunked a petite madeleine and then remembered all that he remembered. The fountain is by Vigoureux."

Bill turned to the center of the square and the fountain. "Who's that up in it?"

"The Virgin Mary, by the sculptor Merlieux."

"It's just not normal, the things you keep in your head."

"Why are you here, Bill? Of all places, here? In Paris? How is it possible? Are you on vacation?"

"One of my reporters has gone missing. His name is Julio. A bit of a strange bird. Ever heard of him? Nobody seems to know what it's about. I guess he's gone haywire. Maybe he doesn't have the chops. Maybe he doesn't have what it takes to do the work. He said he'd be all right in Marseille. Now he has a lot of explaining to do."

Julio said, "Everything's fine."

"The hell it is. Get out of the kitchen. Ever heard this? Words of wisdom. If you can't stand the heat, get the hell out. In our handbook, this is number two. What's number one? Number one is to be honest and up front about goddamn everything with your editor. I have a personal interest in the Marseille assignment. I have an interest in seeing you through it. I should not tell you such things but maybe it will motivate you. I know how journalists are."

"When did Amy tell you?"

"What's that?"

"When did you and Amy discuss me?"

Bill narrowed his eyes. He was looking at Julio in that way again that Julio could not stand, like Bill was trying to figure him out, but Bill wouldn't be able to, he didn't have a knack for it, not like Julio did, not like José María did—and in this moment a number of things inside Julio's head that had been floating, flitting, swooping, like insects over grass, all of these collided and fused so suddenly and so clearly into a revelation: José María had said *in your own house* and Amy did not want him to talk to José María, it seemed she feared he would learn something, and how much had his work, his absence, hurt Amy?—and Bill had come to him at the marble cemetery and here, too, Bill had come, all the way to Paris, with Amy, and did all of this—didn't all of this?—lead directly now to an imagined scene in which Amy told Bill what had happened to Julio, what he'd done, where he was, and Bill took her hand in an attitude of sympathy, or was it something other than sympathy, and then Bill and Amy leaned together, they moved to one another, they moved closer, and Amy looked up at Bill, and then what? Was it possible that they had then kissed? Wasn't it possible then that this had not been the first kiss? Isn't this what José María had been trying to tell him? José María had given him plenty of clues!

Julio grabbed Bill by the collar and hollered at him, "*You!* José María told me! You—*and Amy!*" He tried to choke him, but Bill broke away and ran out of the square. Julio could not pursue him— he could not leave this place, the Square Jean-XXIII, not yet. Out of breath, he dropped onto the bench.

࿔

Uniformed police appeared and walked through. Someone must've told them there had been violence. But of course all was calm now, only Julio could not open his hands, there was still the rise of the anger inside of him, and so he did not move. He knew if the police approached him that he might not be able to stop himself from doing something, whether it would be rushing the police and hollering at them like he had at Bill, or whether it would be taking the twelve long running steps to the fence and up over it and down into the Seine—any of these things might happen. But nothing happened, only the police walked through the Square Jean-XXIII and around the center where there stood black tulips and the high *la Fontaine de la Vierge* and higher up the cathedral in the sky, and they looked at everyone, looking at the tourists taking pictures and the tourists resting in the shade, and looking too at Julio, this man alone on a bench, who probably seemed to them like everyone else. And then the police were gone.

ॐ

Julio saw Amy come the way he had expected, from the direction Bill had fled—"Naturally," he said to himself—she appeared coming cautiously from along the side of the cathedral, looking ahead for him. When she saw him at the same spot under the trees, she would not come closer, she would not come all the way under the shade of the trees. She wiped her eyes. She'd been crying. She called out to him, desperate, imploring, "I should've told you but it seemed too dangerous!"

He was shaking. "You and Bill. José María told me!"

"No, Julio, listen to me! José María is gone. You know this!"

"He told me! What you've been up to! Now go away! Go away!" He couldn't trust what he might do. His hands would not open, and now she was between him and the fence where he could go over and down into the Seine.

She clutched at her heart. "Julio!" She was sobbing. "He wasn't here, Julio!"

"He was!"

"He's dead, Julio! He died in Syria. Two years ago!"

"What? What's this?"

"We went to the funeral," she said. "You remember! You must remember. At the church in San Antonio with his family, his sisters, his mother in black. You prayed with his mother. You remember now, don't you? Julio—"

He had his arms over his head. His eyes shut tightly. It was true. He remembered. José María was dead. He'd been killed in Syria, two years ago. Amy's arms were around him now, and he shook with the grief as he leaned into her because there was nothing that was true but her. He told her, he tried to explain, all that Father Travieso had told him, and all that he'd learned in childhood, that there was good in people, that the forces of light would triumph over the dark, that he would come to know this when he grew up; all of this is what he was supposed to have come to know.

ॐ

Julio, home again, of relative sound mind again, in the East Village apartment that he and Amy had found together five years ago. They'd bought it after they were married, at a time when they could not afford it, and still now after five years they could not afford it. The truth was that they could and they couldn't. Things were always in constant need of repair, the plumbing, the electrical, the fixtures, the floors, the windows. The place was a financial burden, both the apartment and the city were a financial burden, but somehow every month they managed to pay the minimum amounts that were due. They had a lot of debt but they had enough to get by. They didn't have children to provide for. To many people it would seem that they had plenty. To many it would seem that they were privileged to be in New York City, to be doing the work that they did. Julio would agree with this. He did not want to live somewhere else if he would be doing different work. Money was not as important to him as what he did for a living, not by a long shot.

Today, Amy left for the office ahead of him because she had early meetings. Julio took his time. He organized his equipment. He cleaned lenses. At the desk in the front room he opened the laptop and plugged in its external drives. He browsed lists of files. Lists of video assets like ants scrolled down the screen and seemed to continue down onto his hands. He shook out his hands and then, behind him in the hall, a floorboard creaked. It prompted Julio to stand from the chair at the desk in the front room. He knew that no one was there. He walked into the hall with the old floor creaking under his every step, and he walked past the doorway to the narrow kitchen, past the apartment front door, and past the one closet and the bathroom, and into the bedroom, where it was the other room— a home of two rooms: the front room, the bedroom. It was not a walk through the apartment. It was taking a few steps from here to there. Outside the windows were brick walls of the next apartment building, with the gangly metal work of fire escapes, and other people's windows with air conditioners propped up by a wood block or by an old kitchen drawer.

Everywhere inside the apartment the things that he and Amy owned were crammed into corners, under furniture, on bookshelves, in kitchen cabinets and drawers. In such a place as this tiny apartment, things had to be stored wherever there happened to be space. Things did not belong in a given room. Things were not grouped. Things were scattered. To misplace something meant not to set it down in the wrong place, but instead to lose track of it. When something was misplaced it could take hours to find it.

Endlessly Julio and Amy were occupied with organizing things, stacking, piling, shelving, containing, while always after some time chaos again overcame order, and somehow none of it mattered, it had simply become their way of living. Their lives, though, were not of this apartment. This apartment could disappear from their lives and they would simply find another. The essence of who they were was not the apartment. They would not mind one day finding themselves in another apartment. Their lives were as much of the East Village, of New York City, and of all the places they had seen and come from.

Julio knew that no one else was in the apartment and he found this to be true. The hall floorboard creak had startled him in the way that an event which one expected to happen would in fact happen when there was really no indication that it would. Like when the woman stopped him on his way out of Marseille, the woman for whom he'd made snow fall on rue Carnot, the woman who ran up to him when he was leaving and bade him stop at the edge of the Cours Julien square and shoved paper into a pocket of his suitcase. Somehow at the time he'd known that she would want to say something to him before he left Marseille. Or maybe what he remembered of that moment was not the same as what had happened. Maybe he hadn't known that she would want to say something to him, that she would find him before he left in the way that she in fact had.

Even now, he could not trust his impressions of that time. The therapist woman, whom he was now seeing as a matter of course, had told him that the accuracy of his memory didn't matter. There would be no repair of damaged experience. She'd said that she was not a miracle worker. There would be new experiences. The thing to do was to make him well.

José María's ghost had not visited again. Sometimes Julio imagined, though he did not really see, José María sitting next to the therapist and making a show of agreeing with whatever it was that she said. José María was sometimes very amused by what she said. It was obvious stuff. Anyone might've said what she was saying. Indeed, José María could hardly contain his laughter. And there were somber moments. Sometimes Julio imagined, though it was not real, that José María regarded him from a great distance through a camera lens, framing him. José María then turned to the work of writing, reporting, exposing story, shaping its narrative, as was the way of their work. But in truth José María had not visited again. Probably the pills kept him at bay.

Julio in the kitchen checked the pillbox to make sure that he hadn't forgotten to take today's pills. He could not easily lose track of these pills. The pillbox sat on a kitchen shelf at eye level. Dishes and other things had been moved away to open up a clear and evident space for the pillbox. He and Amy had worked all of this out. Like anything else, like shaving in the mirror, it only required a daily routine and room enough in everyday life for it to recur.

He found that today he had taken the day's pills. He had not misplaced the pillbox, or anything else. Except for the paper the woman had shoved into his suitcase. He had misplaced it. What had he done with that?

It took some time but when he found the paper, which was in a closet with the suitcase, still in the suitcase pocket just where he had not expected it to be, he unrolled the paper gently. It was a sketch, penciled on an irregular scrap. It was paper torn away from the corner of something much bigger. The few words printed on the back of it led him to believe that it had been a real estate advertisement pasted up on a wall. The paper had creases from where it had been pinched in the pocket. After all, it had traveled in the suitcase pocket for thousands of miles. In an odd corner, there was what at first seemed merely a scrawl, but after some study Julio believed it to be the artist's signature, a wide and sweeping letter R.

The paper would not lie open and flat on the desk. It had learned its rolled shape and could not be convinced to change for him, for the convenience of allowing him to stand back and look at it. But there was a kind of magic putty that he and Amy had discovered years ago for the purpose of fixing a piece of paper to a wall. He found the putty in the desk drawer and rolled each of four beads of putty between his fingers and thumb and then gently between his palms. He pressed these beads of putty on the back of the sketch at the four corners, and then put the sketch up on the wall, where it stuck. He stepped back to give it a good look.

He was transported.

Acknowledgements

I am deeply grateful to a huge number of people for encouragement and confidence in my pursuit of this book.

Chief among them my wife, the love of my life, truly, Paige Sellers. And my editor Betsy Maury for guiding my voice and shepherding these stories. My publisher Aileen Cassinetto, for embracing this book, believing in it, and guiding it into publication so gracefully. For generous early notes and counsel, my dear friend Joseph Salvatore. Another dear friend, my literary collaborator Sylvie Bertrand, for suggesting that I visit Marseille. And Claire and Pierre, and Arianne Dorval and Babouche, and the countless souls of Marseille who moved me deeply, Philip Cartelli, Borja the Spaniard, Katerina, Michel, Nicholas, Bernadette, Samira, in this city where, as Jean-Claude Izzo wrote, "even to lose you have to know how to fight."

ABOUT THE AUTHOR

Christopher X. Shade is co-founder and co-editor of *Cagibi*, at cagibilit.com, a journal of poetry and prose. His stories and book reviews have appeared widely, and he has won story awards including the 2016 Writers at Work fellowship competition. He teaches fiction and poetry writing at The Writers Studio. Raised in the South, he now lives with his wife in New York City.

Established in 2016, **PALOMA PRESS** is a San Francisco Bay Area-based independent literary press publishing poetry, prose, and limited edition books. Titles include *BLUE* by Wesley St. Jo & Remé Grefalda (officially launched at The Library of Congress in September 2017), and *MANHATTAN: An Archaeology* by Eileen R. Tabios (which debuted at the 4th Filipino American International Book Festival at the San Francisco Public Library).

Paloma Press believes in the power of the literary arts, how it can create empathy, bridge divides, change the world. To this end, Paloma has released fundraising chapbooks such as *MARAWI*, in support of relief efforts in the Southern Philippines; and *AFTER IRMA AFTER HARVEY*, in support of hurricane-displaced animals in Texas, Florida and Puerto Rico. As part of the San Francisco Litquake Festival, Paloma proudly curated the wildly successful literary reading, "THREE SHEETS TO THE WIND," and raised money for the Napa Valley Community Disaster Relief Fund. In 2018, the fundraising anthology, *HUMANITY*, was released in support of UNICEF's Emergency Relief campaigns on the borders of the United States and in Syria.